D0210437

# BLOOD ON A BLUE MOON

## A Sheaffer Blue Mystery

## Jessica H. Stone

# BLOOD ON A BLUE MOON

## A Sheaffer Blue Mystery

## Jessica H. Stone

Sidekick Press
Bellingham, Washington
United States of America

Publisher's Note: This is a work of fiction. Names, characters, places, and incidents are a product of the author's imagination. Locales and public names are sometimes used for atmospheric purposes. Any resemblance to actual people, living or dead, or to businesses, companies, events, institutions, or locales is coincidental.

Sidekick Press
2950 Newmarket Street
Suite 101-329
Bellingham, Washington 98226
www.sidekickpress.com


Blood on a Blue Moon/Jessica H. Stone

ISBN 978-1-7344945-7-0
LCCN 2020925456

*Dedicated to*
*Denise*

## The First Full Moon

The spider danced. Eight hairy legs—each laced into a purple high-top Converse sneaker—moved in a slow shuffle. Its bowler hat, cocked at a jaunty angle, bobbed with every step. If it hadn't been for the circus music, I would have missed the entire performance. It was the music—the lively tinkle of the calliope calling folks to the big top—that made me open one eye in time to catch the tap-dancing arachnid in motion.

The beam from my alarm clock threw a spotlight on the spider, a smiling unicorn, three black roses, and Jesus flashing a peace symbol. The body art, along with several other designs, moved with the involuntary flexing of the muscled arm draped over my shoulder. The music stopped, but I knew it would start again. Soon. I groaned and pushed against the warm body snugged to mine. He rolled over with a grunt.

I turned and watched him for a moment. Shaggy hair flopped soft around his face. Surfer boy blond. Even after a full year in the Pacific Northwest, and even in the clock's green digital light, he still managed to glow with a deep California tan.

We'd met the day before during a Groupon coupon event. For twenty-four dollars I received an introductory paddleboard lesson and, as it turned out, an evening of advanced lessons—private lessons—with the young instructor. I started to shake my head and stopped. The motion hurt. Did we really empty the whole fifth of Jack Daniel's?

Jamie—or wait—maybe it was Jimmy. Or Jeff? No, maybe not a "J" name at all. Kevin? His lips formed a small "o" and puckered in little bubble blowing motions. I smiled. I couldn't remember his name but I certainly remembered how delicious those lips had been a few hours earlier.

The music started again. "Shit." I knew I had to answer the phone. My boss, Glen Broom, would keep calling, and that stupid circus music would continue, until I picked up. I gave old man Broom that ringtone because, like so many of my bosses, the guy was a clown. A certifiable joke. Whenever he called me, my life became a circus.

I didn't like my boss and didn't like my job. The truth is, I rarely liked any of my jobs or any of my bosses—and I'd had a lot of both. I figured that if I could just stay employed long enough to save the bucks to repair my blown headsail, fix the generator, and fill my cruising kitty, I'd stuff my boat full of beef jerky, saltine crackers, and Tennessee whiskey. Then I'd sail *Ink Spot* up from Seattle and through the Strait of Juan de Fuca. We'd round the corner at Cape Flattery, hang a left, and head on down the coast. Wouldn't stop until we made it to Zihuatanejo, Mexico. Then I'd drop anchor and spend my days sleeping in a hammock and my nights dancing with dark-eyed men. That's all I wanted. Was that so much to ask? I kept thinking it should be a piece of cake; but once again, it was harder to break free than I'd imagined.

I thought maybe this job would be different. After all, the clown hadn't even hinted at firing me, and it had already been six weeks. Three weeks longer than my last job at *Roger's Roadkill Cleanup "You smash 'em we scrape 'em,"* and a full month longer than my stint as the only female bouncer at the *All Naked Live Girls Review* on First Avenue. I held onto that hope—yeah, maybe this job would be the one to fund my getaway.

I glanced at Kurt, or maybe he was Randy, or Ray. Finally, I gave up trying to remember his name and decided to call him "Spiderman," after his silly tattoo. I also decided to give him a kiss. He made a burbling sound as my lips brushed his cheek. His skin smelled of sunshine and sex.

I figured the clown would wait a full four minutes before he punched redial. I slid off the bunk and slipped in a pool of something slick. *Bam!* Fell flat on my bare ass. It took a moment for me to catch my breath and to find and recap the bottle of coconut oil that had been so handy earlier. With a groan, I clutched the side of the bunk, pulled myself to standing, swayed a moment, and then stumbled into *Ink Spot's* salon. I flicked the nav station's tiny red light.

My boat was a total mess. It was never what you'd call tidy. I was a bit of a slob—okay, a big slob. Still, this was extreme. It looked like we'd been in a major storm at sea. Maybe even turned turtle or at least broached. Clothes, magazines, miscellaneous boat parts, and a shovel from my road clean-up gig were cluttered in tangled confusion. My extensive collection of adult toys was scattered across the salon table. I grimaced. We must have had more fun than I remembered.

I searched the wreckage for my phone and found the JD bottle under a pizza box. The box was empty, but there was still a swig of whiskey left. I finished it off—good as mouthwash. When the first notes of the music started up again, I followed the sound to my jacket which lay crumpled on the floor by the galley sink. The phone hid underneath it, nesting in the left cup of my favorite black bra. I snatched my cell and glanced at the time. Crap—0530. Obviously, I wasn't late for work.

"Blue here."

"Sheaffer, I've told you a million times to keep the phone by your bed. It's our responsibility to be available to our clients 24/7. They depend on us. It's what we're known for—*City Wide Insurance. Dependable and Reliable. Always Ready When You Need Us.* Remember? What took you so long to answer this time?"

The clown went through the same routine every time he called me. He knew his little insurance company could never be a good neighbor, but he reasoned that, at least, we could be there. His spiel irritated me. Still, I'd learned that if I mumbled something—anything—he'd move on. So, I mumbled and he went on.

"Listen Sheaffer. I need you to go to an incident right now." Broom called every issue in the insurance busi-

ness, big or small, an incident. At City Wide, most issues were small. "There's been a fire on one of the Lake
Union docks—a houseboat fire. I want you to get there
while the media are still around. Be sure to make a presence. Be sure we're mentioned in the police report."

He rattled on in that voice that sounded like he was
reporting a falling sky or another 9/11. I tuned him out
and searched for something to wear. The plastic box
where I stored my underpants was empty. That meant
two things—one of these days I'd have to do laundry,
and today would be a day without panties. I bent to retrieve my jeans from under the table and noticed a
shimmery trail sliding down my inner thigh.

"Sheaffer, are you listening to me?" The clown
sounded panicky.

"Um, yeah...." I lifted a T-shirt from the settee. It was
inside out. I turned it right-side out and noticed the
logo—*Surf Ballard*. I grinned, flipped it inside out and
wiped my leg. It would be dry before he woke and the
scent would be a sexy little reminder. Better, I figured,
than a business card.

"Sheaffer! Are you sure you have the address?"

"Um...." I looked for a pen, found a capless Sharpie in
the sink. "Give it to me again, okay?"

The clown repeated the number and street name. I
wrote it on my palm.

"So, you should be there in about fifteen minutes.
Get as much information as you can and be sure everyone sees you're on the job. Be sure the media sees that
City Wide is there. Then come straight to the office and
fill me in. Sheaffer, you got that?"

"Yeah, got it." I crunched the phone between my cheek and shoulder and tugged at my jeans. As a charter member of "Club Cellulite," I've always struggled into jeans, but this morning they were extra tight. I made a mental note to ease off on the late-night pizza. I stopped tugging for a minute. Something bugged me because this sounded like a typical gig. Broom was always sending me out to investigate minor insurance incidents—small fires, fender benders, reports of laptops and cameras "stolen" from cars. Standard insurance stuff—nothing that required this frantic predawn action.

"Ah, one question, boss. So, it's a houseboat fire. Probably one of those old ones. They're all wood, you know. Probably just faulty wiring or something. Why the hurry?"

The clown fell silent a moment. I could imagine him holding his breath, his face swelling and turning ripe strawberry. He lit into me.

"You *haven't* been listening. It's a houseboat fire, yes. And it was an old, wooden houseboat, yes. And you have to know that our most important client owns most of that dock, and she insures the property with us." He paused and gulped for air.

I could almost see him shaking and clenching and unclenching his fists. The man was seriously over-wound.

"Besides all that, as I already told you, this isn't simply a fire. This time, there's a body."

# 2

Lawrence Winslow lathered his chest with the creamy shower gel his wife had bought for him. Thick suds slid down his torso. He sucked in, held his breath, and rubbed his hand over his muscles, wet and slick. Not bad for seventy-one. Maybe not skinny the way he'd been in college, but trim, tight, and healthy. No old man paunch like most of the men in his position. They hid the signs of age under expensive suits the way their wives disguised weight under designer clothing. Lawrence smiled. His wife, thirty years his junior, didn't need to hide anything. She was, by anyone's standards, stunning. So what if she could be a royal pain—cold and demanding. He was the envy of every man who ever saw her. And so what if she used surgery and spas to enhance her natural beauty. He could afford any treatment she selected and besides, it kept her busy—out of his hair.

Lawrence hummed bits of a tune from the show he and Beverly had seen the night before. He smiled again. They'd shared a private box with Bill and Melinda. Bill and Melinda. Nice couple. *Long way up the food chain, Larry Boy*, he thought. *Long way up the ladder.* He stretched and slid his hand lower through the foam. Nothing like a slow Sunday morning.

Beverly Winslow stood on the redwood deck that wrapped around the 4.5-million-dollar home that Lawrence built. The deck offered views of Lake Washington, the University, Mount Rainier, and the rivers of money that flowed down the streets of their community. She curled her left hand around a cup of freshly brewed espresso. A unique blend of beans, a gift from the CEO of Starbucks himself. She balanced a thin imported cigarette between the fingers of her right hand. Coffee steam and cigarette smoke spiraled in the pale, teal-colored light of Chihuly glass.

Beverly liked smoking. Mostly because Lawrence hated her habit. She thought about his rants and felt smug. He whined about all the health risks. He said nobody except Japanese businessmen, European diplomats, and the lower class smoked anymore. What about the second-hand smoke risk to him? And the smell!

She took a long, slow pull on the cigarette. Smoking was one of the few things she and her mother agreed on. Botox stopped a frown as she thought of her mother, Elaine. The two rarely got along. Didn't even like each other. Of course, no one would ever have guessed that. To the players in their social circles—the ones who mattered anyway—Beverly and her mother were inseparable. She exhaled. Coughed. Sipped her espresso.

A soft buzzing sound from the kitchen counter distracted her. Her husband's cell phone vibrated with an incoming call. Beverly glanced at the clock—too early on a Sunday morning for anyone to call. Strange. She waited until the vibrating stopped and the message light flashed. She picked up the phone and tapped in her husband's code.

"An advantage of older men," she'd told a girlfriend, "is that they're clueless when it comes to technology. You have to set everything up for them, and you know all their passwords." She listened, bored, to the first two saved messages. Work calls. The third caught her attention.

"Larry, this is Shirley. Long time and all that." The voice was definitely that of an older woman. But it didn't crack or scratch. It was deep and low and sexy. "So, my old friend, it seems we have a little unfinished business. I'm still at the same place, and I know you have my number." The call ended.

Beverly stubbed out her cigarette and spun toward the door. The heels of her eight-hundred-dollar mules clicked against Italian marble. Her black satin robe flapped like a great shining wing. It took her exactly three minutes to fly through the house and up the stairs to the bedroom.

She pushed into the master bath, took two strides to the shower, grabbed the curved glass handle on the shower door and yanked it open so fast foam flew from her husband's body.

She ignored the grip Larry had on himself. Beverly clenched her fists and spat her words.

"Who the hell is Shirley?"

# 3

Spiderman was harder to get out of bed than in. We burned a half hour in the process, a delightful half hour for sure, but when he finally plied his skateboard down the dock, I was dangerously late. I squirmed back into my jeans, pulled on the first T-shirt I could find, and grabbed my denim jacket and day pack. I left *Ink Spot* unlocked. Always figured marinas—especially funky little marinas like Ballard Mill—were safe.

Of course, it was raining. And of course, that meant the two parking tickets plastered to the windshield of Roger, my 1978 Volvo station wagon, were blurred and gummy. Roger's locks had failed years ago, but that didn't bother me because it only took a special kick—in the right spot—to open the driver's door. I kicked, it creaked open, and I slid in. I peeled off the strip of duct tape holding the glove compartment closed and crammed the soggy tickets in with all the others. I vowed that someday I'd clean my car and recycle all that useless paper issued by the City of Seattle.

I took a moment to check myself in Roger's rearview mirror. Not a pretty sight. I ran my fingers through my hair and applied a slick of berry-tinted lip balm to my mouth and cheeks. Okay. Better. In a final quick look, I realized the T-shirt I'd grabbed was not the most professional choice. The old shirt was a faded souvenir from one of Seattle's infamous public relations snafus. It advertised the brilliant idea of some bored city planner: A trolley car that didn't go anywhere, cost taxpayers a ton of money, and was given a name that amused tourists and embarrassed local politicians. The project was called the South Lake Union Trolley. My T-shirt read—*Ride the S.L.U.T.* I realized it wouldn't look all that great in crime scene photos, and it definitely wouldn't give the impression my boss wanted. I buttoned my jacket. Ready to roll, I gently patted the dashboard.

"Okay, Roger, old boy, favorite car of mine." I turned the key. Nothing happened. "Oh, come on now, buddy, let's take a little drive together." Another try. Again, nothing. "Damn it! Start, you piece of shit." I smacked the dashboard. Roger roared to life.

Two fire trucks blocked the narrow unpaved street running in front of the address I'd written on my palm. An ambulance parked between the fire trucks sat waiting—its back doors opened wide—its rotating dome light slowly illuminating the scene. Red, then white. Red, then white. Cop cars clogged the rest of the parking area. I circled the block twice and then stashed Roger in a no-parking zone three blocks away. By the time I made it back to the scene, I was soaked.

Eight long docks jetted into Lake Union to form a neighborhood of floating sidewalks and single-family dwellings. A whitewashed sign with faded blue lettering welcomed visitors to the gatehouse of Dock W—a dock that tread water in the middle of this soggy community. Because of the pounding rain, the customary group of early morning joggers and dog-walkers who would usually stop to catch a glimpse of someone else's misery had dwindled to a small pod of vagrants—Seattle's regulars. They huddled together under the weathered shelter and mumbled to each other.

I stepped inside the gatehouse, shook the rain from my jacket, and rummaged through my day pack for a baseball cap. Twisting my wet hair into a makeshift ponytail, I jammed it through the opening in the back of the cap and started down the sketchy wooden steps that led from the gatehouse to the dock below. A stretch of black and yellow crime-scene tape blocked the way, and two uniformed cops draped in clear plastic ponchos stood sentinel at the foot of the stairs.

Because of the many odd jobs I'd held over the years, I knew almost everyone who served on the force—men and women alike. Firefighters, too. Theirs was a small community populated with strong, healthy, almost fearless folk who lived in danger and partied like it might be their last. Actually, in their line of work, every day, and every party very well *could* have been their last. I called down to one of the cops. "Hey there, officer, let a girl do her job?"

He turned, looked up, grinned, and waved me through. I ducked under the tape, gripped the handrail and jumped the steps, two at a time.

"So, my favorite redheaded sailor-girl." The cop gave a teasing smile. "When do I get to go swimming off that boat of yours?"

I returned the grin and whispered, "When are you gonna learn to hold your breath, officer?"

He laughed at our private joke and winked as I walked past.

Although I'd lived most of my adult life in marinas, I'd never visited a houseboat community. So, despite being wet, chilled, and hung over, I was intrigued. The dock wobbled under my steps. Gray planks warped in different directions, gaps between them gave peeks at the olive water below, splats of seagull poop puddled every few feet, and now and then, a hearty little weed found a way to grow in dirty patches of rotting wood. The smell of smoke hung thick in the morning fog.

I paused for a moment and scanned the scene. The floating neighborhood was a jumble of styles and de-signs, a study in architectural anachronism. No two houseboats even remotely resembled each other. I passed a three-story structure painted glossy white. Next to it, a squat, unpainted building listed to port. The pontoon on its left side lacked flotation, and it looked as if it might sink at any moment. I imagined the folks in the white houseboat prayed it would.

Across the dock, a two-story redwood structure sat pretty and neat. Stained glass colored every window, flowerpots bursting with color lined the porch, and a triangle-shaped rainbow flag dripped rain and pride. As I passed, I could hear several small dogs yapping behind the front door.

A mishmash of culture and conditions lent a certain charm to this little community. The place had a friendly "you can trust me" vibe that made me wish I'd found it under different circumstances.

I lowered my head and continued. Not paying attention, I almost smacked into a blue plastic tarp that stretched at eye level across the dock between two houseboats. I stopped short and looked up.

Two elderly women, each wrapped in a blanket, stood under the tarp on the deck of a small pink home. One wore a yellow plastic shower cap patterned with ducks cavorting in bathtubs. She held a plastic container filled with cookies. The other wore a transparent rain bonnet tied in a bow under her chin. I glanced down and noticed red plaid boots sticking out from under her blanket.

She smiled at me. "Coffee, dear?" She pointed to a card table and a large thermos.

The thermos beckoned. I ducked under the tarp. "Yes, I'd love that." My teeth chattered and my hands trembled as I accepted the steaming mug.

"Cookie? Pulled them from the oven a few minutes ago." The woman in the shower cap held the box toward me. I took a sip of coffee, felt the liquid warm all the way down.

"No, but thank you. This is perfect." With the gift that only coffee—strong black coffee—can give, I felt myself coming back to reality from a night of way too much fun.

The women watched me for a moment, and then the lady in the plaid boots tilted her head slightly. "Are you with the fire department, dear?"

"No." I shook my head—tested for pain—felt pretty good.

"Oh, she's a nurse, Dot, anyone can see that. Maybe Shirley needs some medicine. Maybe she's not...."

Her friend laid one hand on the woman's arm to stop her. "She is gone, Geraldine. She really is gone." She searched the other woman's face. Geraldine appeared more befuddled than sad. Her friend turned to me.

"I'm sorry dear, we didn't introduce ourselves." She nodded to the woman with the cookies. "This is Geraldine. You have to excuse her; sometimes she gets...well, she gets a little confused." She paused and looped her arm around her friend for a quick hug. Geraldine nodded as if in agreement and smiled. Her friend continued. "I'm Dorothy. This..." she turned and gestured toward the houseboat behind them, "is my home." She turned back to me. "Are you with the coroner's office, then?"

"No." I smiled and held out my hand to Dorothy. "Blue. Sheaffer Blue. I'm an investigator with City Wide Insurance."

"Oh my, an insurance investigator," Geraldine said. "Such a big fancy job for such a young girl."

I started to explain that it wasn't so fancy and that thirty wasn't so young but stopped when I noticed three men approach. I recognized one of them—a tall under-cover cop that I'd had some under-the-covers fun with a few months earlier. A man dressed in a drab green jacket scurried to keep up. He carried a medical bag. Coroner, I figured. The third guy wore a tailored black leather jacket. He held a briefcase over his head as a makeshift umbrella, hiding his face. He walked with a limp. The three men ducked under the tarp and moved past without glancing at me, or the ladies with their offerings of hot coffee and warm cookies.

"Ladies, I'm sorry I can't stay and chat. I need to get to the scene before they remove the body." My words landed like a slap. The women shrunk back. Geraldine's lower lip quivered. I gave myself a hard mental kick in the butt. It was obvious that the deceased was a dear friend or at least a well-liked neighbor. "I'm so sorry. I didn't mean..." Embarrassed, I leaned over to put the mug on the table.

"That's alright, dear," Dorothy said. Her voice was strong and steady and filled with sorrow. She glanced at the mug. "Take it with you. The coffee will keep you warm. Return it when you leave. Set it on the stoop if we're not out here."

I thanked them for the second time, ducked from under the tarp's protection and hurried after the men. Despite the thick cloud cover, a soft blue light welcomed the day. I couldn't see the actual site of the fire, yet even with all the rain, I could smell it. My nose crinkled with the reek of burned wood, wet ash, and smoldering garbage—strong, slightly acidic, rancid.

When I caught up with them, my cop buddy and the man in the green jacket were hunched over a body bag lying on a stretcher. The guy in the leather coat stood on the porch of the smoldering houseboat, his back to us. The stench here was strong. The same mix of charred wood and garbage I'd noticed earlier combined with the distinct smell of barbecued ribs. I glanced down—big mistake. The bag was unzipped. I breathed through my mouth and willed myself not to retch. I looked away and focused on a Coast Guard skiff making its early morning rounds.

"Can't do much here," the man with the doctor's bag said. "Too wet. Let's get her into the ambulance. I can do a quick exam there, but best to take her to the lab."

My buddy, the undercover cop, nodded at two EMTs. "Okay," he said, "take her." He leaned over and zipped the bag shut. When he straightened, he noticed me and his face went from somber to bright. "Sheaffer! What a pleasant surprise." He held out his hand. "Didn't expect to see you this early in the day—or are you still on your way home?"

I smiled. "Official business officer. *City Wide Insurance. Dependable and Reliable. Always Ready When You Need Us.*" I rattled off the stupid jingle, then paused. "Although," I shuddered, "I have to admit, this is my first burned body. Actually, my first body."

"Well, always nice to see you, Blue. No matter what brings you out. We should hook up later this week. Yeah?"

"Thanks. Maybe." I bit my lip; something was missing. "So, uh, Greg." I took a stab at remembering his name. "Where is the press? I thought King 5 News would be all over this."

He grimaced. "Here and gone. First responders gave them a few lines when they arrived, let them do a little filming, and then escorted them to the street. That's the reason for leaving the body inside until now. Respect for the deceased. And besides, the public doesn't need to see that." He cleared his throat. "And, it's Gary." Maybe to hide his embarrassment, or mine, he turned toward the houseboat.

"Hey Dave, I'm heading back to the lab with the doc. We need to get some more information. We'll leave a couple of uniforms. They can check IDs, let the locals in and out, and keep the lookie-loos at bay. Meet you at the station?"

The other man turned slowly and with purpose. For the first time, I was able to see his face. Round, clean-shaven, almost a baby face. His eyes dark and intense. He stood about five-five, with straight black hair in a style clearly not from Discount Cuts. I guessed Asian American, educated and moneyed. He offered a curt nod to Gary, his gaze now on me. I squirmed a little, suddenly glad I'd buttoned my jacket, suddenly regretting I'd skipped a shower. Then I mentally chastised myself. *The guy is short, probably a conservative, and probably not much fun—what are you thinking?* I straightened and banished the thought.

"Sheaffer, this is Detective David Chen, Homicide. He's on loan from San Francisco—some kind of PR program—so try to play nice." Gary gestured toward the other man and then to me. "Chen, Blue. Sheaffer Blue, insurance investigator."

David Chen didn't step from the porch or offer to shake hands. He simply gave the same curt nod and turned back to the smoldering houseboat.

"Homicide?" His title threw me. "Why a homicide detective? What makes anyone think homicide?" I said. Except for the smoke curling up in fat tendrils from the soaked wood, and the rancid smell, the floating dock seemed peaceful and safe. If it hadn't been smack-dab in the middle of downtown Seattle, it could have been a street in any small town, USA. Could have been a street named Oak or Chestnut or Main. A street with a church at one end and a bakery at the other. A slice of 1950s American Pie.

Gary shrugged. "Might not be. The victim was an old woman. Maybe she fell asleep or just fell and couldn't get up. Never mind. You do your insurance thing. This will probably be a pretty simple case for you because the place is completely trashed. It will have to be towed and destroyed. No dispute. Full payout if the old gal had insurance. Not sure, though, about her family. We're still checking."

I frowned. "Well, Greg...um, Gary, keep me in the loop if you find anything I can use?"

"Always." He turned and took off down the dock behind the EMTs carrying the stretcher with the long, black body bag. I noticed he didn't mention hooking up again.

# 4

Elaine Dupont crossed one tanned leg over the other, leaned back in the fake leather chair and clicked her gold lighter. She drew a long pull on the Dunhill, tilted her head ever so slightly, and blew a stream of smoke toward the ceiling.

Glen Broom coughed and glanced at the NO SMOKING sign prominently displayed on the wall by the door.

Elaine raised one eyebrow. "I'll wait while you look for that file. And, of course, I'll need an ashtray."

"Yes, of course, Mrs. Dupont." Broom wrung his hands. "It will only take a minute to get the file, and I'll, um, find something for you. Excuse me a moment." He avoided another look at the sign as he scurried from the room.

Elaine allowed a thin smile. Unlike her daughter, she did not enjoy smoking all that much but, like a cat with a beetle, she enjoyed taunting her victims. And today, Glen Broom, owner of this tacky little one-off insurance agency, was her victim. Nothing upset the ever-so-green and oh-so-socially-conscious Seattleite more than a smoker. Ordinary citizens who lit up indoors, or even within hiking distance of a Seattle business, were immediately ostracized and perhaps issued a police warning. Elaine Dupont, however, was no ordinary citizen. She was well aware that the policies she carried with Broom's agency made up the majority of his accounts. This gave her control, and Elaine enjoyed control.

Broom returned with a stack of manila folders and a chipped coffee mug. He placed it on the corner of his desk in front of her. "I'm sorry," he said. "We don't have any ashtrays. This is mine. Feel free."

Elaine leaned forward, turned the mug around and glanced at its logo. Purple script spelled out "Foster School of Business—MBA Program." She looked at a remaining swirl of coffee. She shrugged and dropped her still lit cigarette into the mug—the cigarette hissed. Broom grimaced but moved on.

"I've checked, and you are, of course, correct. And, of course, it's all over the news." He pulled a file from the stack. "I sent our top agent out to investigate. She's there now, working with the police. Rest assured, Mrs. Dupont, we are on this and will have it wrapped up quickly, just as you wish." As he said the words, Glen Broom sent out a silent prayer. *Please, please let Sheaffer be there.*

"Good," Elaine said. "Only three more units outstanding, right?"

Broom swallowed and nodded. Small beads of sweat dotted his forehead. He hoped she didn't notice.

"So, tell me. Who gets the insurance money on this one?" Elaine leaned forward and fixed her stare at Broom. This was so easy.

"Well, now, of course, you know that I can't say anything at this time. Privacy laws and…" It took all he had to avoid reaching up to swipe at the sweat.

"I suppose I could find out through other means," Elaine said. "But that might take time, and you know how I hate to waste time. Of course, if I can't get what I want from this agency…"

Broom caved. He swiped his forehead then wiped his damp hand on his slacks. Out of habit, he reached for his mug. Smoke swirled over the rim. He sneezed.

Elaine started to stand.

"Oh, well I'm sure…" Broom returned the mug to the desk. "Perhaps in this one case…" Elaine smiled and settled back down.

"If it was an accident, the case will go to probate because the deceased didn't have any next of kin." He wrung his hands and started to pace. Realizing how nervous that made him look, he plopped into his desk chair.

"Another beneficiary?" Elaine's eyes narrowed.

"Ah, I did try, several times, to get her to name someone but she refused. Or forgot."

"Well, what happens if there are no beneficiaries?"

Broom pressed his hands flat on top of the folder to control his shaking. "If we can't find a beneficiary and if it was an accident, the case would go to probate."

"Probate!" Elaine sat very straight. "That will take months. I don't want this to take months." She leaned forward and pointed one long finger at Broom. "I have a lot of money riding on this property, so you had better find another solution."

Broom shook his head—he felt dizzy and ill. He hoped it was the thin veil of smoke swirling the room and not a brain aneurysm or some other horror that caused his pain. He took a breath and a chance.

"The only thing is...maybe...if it was suicide, the contract would be null and void. No payment. No probate. The coroner has more control...."

Elaine thought for a moment. Except for the muffled sounds of city traffic, the room was quiet. She curled the fingers of her right hand and studied her manicure. Then she spoke, her voice low, almost a purr. "That poor, poor woman. All alone in that dilapidated, dirty old houseboat. I knew she was depressed when I first spoke to her about selling it. Of course, I didn't know the depth of her depression. Apparently, she knew it was time to let go of that death trap of hers and she knew my offer was more than fair—generous, even. But," Elaine sighed, "change is so hard for the elderly." She waited a beat. "I'm sure you will find a way, Mr. Broom. After all..." she paused and gazed around the small, gray office decorated with University of Washington memorabilia and cheap furniture. "So much is at stake, isn't it?"

Broom smacked his knee hard on the edge of the desk as he tried to get up fast enough to see his client out, but before he could reach her, Elaine waltzed out of the office and slid into the waiting limo. Her driver closed the door.

Glen Broom exhaled. He spun around, dashed back inside, and reached for the phone. *Please, please pick up, Sheaffer. Please pick up.*

**5**

David Chen frowned when I stepped from the dock to the deck of the burned houseboat. "You shouldn't come in here. It's dangerous," he said.

I took another two steps and stood directly in front of him.

"I have a dangerous job," I said. My additional two inches gave me an advantage. He was forced to look up for eye contact. It didn't seem to bother him.

"I'm guessing the most dangerous thing you do on the job is to hide from your boss when you're late for work." He didn't smile—just stood there with a calm, in-control gaze.

His comment stung. I'd been late for almost every job I'd ever had, and on this particular morning, I'd been so late I'd missed the media crews. City Wide would not be in the news, and the clown would be pissed. I needed to do something to make up for it. Getting inside, getting photos of the scene would be a big plus. I pretended to ignore Chen's comment and brushed by.

It was clear to me that other than being soaked from the fire hoses, the neighboring houseboats were unharmed. This one, however, looked in bad shape. The axe-wielding fire crew left the front door in splinters. They'd even smashed through what had been a stunning relief carving of a salmon. The screen door hung from one hinge. I stepped over the threshold and surveyed the interior.

The small dwelling consisted of two rooms and a bathroom. Inside, to the right, a narrow space housed blackened kitchen appliances and the remains of a 1950s-style, aluminum-legged table—its Formica top scarred and bubbled. Heat-cracked and broken dishes filled the sink.

Judging by the charred remains of shelving, a singed futon, and piles of badly burned books, I figured the room must have served as a living room, library, and office. The contents of every drawer in a severely scorched rolltop desk spilled to the floor. I wondered if the disarray was because of the fire, or if the owner had shared my housekeeping habits. I picked my way over the soaked debris covering the floor.

"Who lived here?" I didn't turn to face him when I asked the question.

"One senior citizen. Shirley. Shirley Cantrell." I guessed Chen read from notes he'd taken earlier. He probably knew a lot about this case before he even arrived. He struck me as the kind of guy who does his homework. Probably turns it in early.

"Age?"

"Seventy-four."

"Oh." I was glad he couldn't see my face. I have a soft spot for old people—people like elderly ladies who make coffee and cookies for firefighters and coroners. "Anyone else?" I hoped he couldn't hear my voice falter.

"A cat." He slapped his notebook closed. "Neighbor said she had a cat but no sign of it since I've been here. Probably caught in the fire with its owner. We haven't found the body yet."

"Yeah. Probably caught in the fire." I tried to sound matter-of- fact, though I didn't think I was fooling anyone. Like I said, I have a soft spot for elderly people. And, I have a gaping hole in my heart for animals. My thirty-four-year-old sailboat wasn't exactly a domestic household pet haven. Still, if I could, I'd collect every stray dog, cat, gerbil, pot-bellied pig—you name it—and keep them safe and happy. I'd fill that hole with love and fur.

"Don't touch anything," Chen said.

Though grateful for the mood change, I turned and glared at him. *Detective*, I wanted to say, *I'm a professional. I don't destroy evidence. Getting to the truth is my middle name.* I'd read that line in a cheap mystery novel and always wanted to use it. This seemed as good a time as any. In reality, though, I was about as far away from professional as you could get. I didn't have any training for the job and pretty much faked my way through most of my cases. And so, I held my tongue and tried to convey my disdain with a look.

But Chen either missed the subtlety or ignored it. With gloved hands, he sifted through a stack of papers on the desk and another that covered the floor.

I balanced the coffee mug on a window ledge, shrugged out of my day pack, and rummaged through the stuff that lived in there. I found my camera, one of those little point-and-shoot numbers available in your choice of five fun colors. My choice? Brushed tangerine. Not the most professionally impressive equipment. Still, any photos I could take back to the clown would be a big plus. I knew it would be a drag to look at this destruction on the big computer screen in the office—part of the price I paid for being so late and for having this dismal job in the first place. Chen stood still and watched me, his expression unreadable. I tried to shake a feeling that I couldn't quite identify.

When I'd taken what I hoped would be enough photos, I glanced at Chen and then to the remaining room—the bedroom. "Did she...?"

He nodded. I shuddered. I seriously did not want to see the place where the victim—where Shirley—had died. To stretch the time before entering the room, I tried to strike up a conversation with Chen. "Smoking in bed?"

"We don't know yet. But..." He stopped.

"But what?" I felt a bit miffed. His curt answers and controlled demeanor were starting to bug me. Most of the time the guys I worked with were lighthearted and flirtatious. Not so severe and certainly not so aloof. "But what?" I repeated.

Chen looked at me for a moment and then seemed to come to a decision. "Won't know for sure until the fire inspector turns in his report. According to the neighbors, the deceased wasn't a smoker. So..." he shrugged, "we need to do some more digging."

I had no response, so I frowned, tried to look wise and thoughtful as I walked to the bedroom. Chen followed me.

I took more photos and tried to avoid looking—really looking—at the impression in the burned and water-soaked mattress. Much like the front room, this area appeared to have been trashed. Charred clothing spilled from gaping dresser drawers, and a jumble of what might have been cardboard hatboxes blocked the closet door. Piles of ruined books covered almost every available surface here, too. Shirley must have been an avid reader.

It didn't take long to photograph the small room. I slipped the camera into my pocket and turned to leave, but paused to watch Chen. He stood by the door, his body so rigid he could have been a store mannequin or a museum wax figure. I swear the man was in some kind of trance, yet his eyes were bright and alert as they swept over every surface. They seemed to record each scorched piece of clothing, every burned book, and each broken knickknack. No words, observation only—intense, focused observation. Even though I thought I'd taken a pretty good look around, I was sure that Chen saw things I couldn't even imagine.

I stood transfixed, watching him until the sound of circus music tinkled up from my jacket pocket. "Sorry," I muttered as I grabbed the phone. Chen ignored me. "Blue here."

"Sheaffer. Thank God. Are you there? At the scene?" The clown gulped for air.

"Of course I'm here. You sent me here. To the incident, right?"

He paused for a moment as if thinking about my comment.

"Yes. Yes...well, here's the deal. Get what you can and get back to the office ASAP. We *need* to talk."

"Okay, Glen. But there might be evidence of, you know..." I glanced at Chen. He remained motionless, and I could tell the spell had been broken.

"Evidence of what?" Broom's voice shot up an octave.

"Homicide. *This* might be more than an accident. This might be a *real* incident."

Broom was speechless for a full thirty seconds. Then he muttered something about exploding brain cells. It didn't make any sense to me. Finally, he sighed.

"Well, get here as fast as you can." He paused. I could tell his little mind was churning. "Oh, and Blue?"

"Hmmm?"

"Don't touch anything."

I probably made a face because Chen chuckled, ever so slightly. He took my coffee mug from the window ledge and followed me out of the building and onto the dock.

The rain had stopped and a thin streak of morning light fought its way through the clouds. I took my first deep breath since I'd entered Shirley's home. My lungs expanded until they hurt.

Chen breathed deeply too before he turned to me and handed me the mug. "Fire is my least favorite crime scene. I can't stand the smell."

This was the first time he'd initiated conversation, and it surprised me. I stopped myself right as I was about to say something snarky like, *So, tell me, what is your favorite crime scene?* Maybe he was trying to be nice. I decided to play it straight.

"Do you seriously think this was something other than an accident?" I squinted and shielded my eyes from the sun.

"I don't know." He reached under his leather jacket and pulled a business card from his shirt pocket. He handed it to me. "There isn't anything obvious, yet. But..." He paused a moment, and I thought I saw a flicker of sadness in his eyes. "I have a feeling."

"Thanks." I took the card and slipped it into the back pocket of my jeans. "Have you been doing this a long time? I mean, long enough to trust a feeling?"

He nodded. "Too long. Too many feelings about crime. About murder. Sometimes I wish..." He stopped—maybe embarrassed. "Well, you have my card. Since we're both investigating the same thing, I'd appreciate it if you'd contact me if you stumble across anything of interest."

*Stumble across?* I thought about his word choice. I wasn't sure if he was putting me down or if it was his version of casual. I decided I didn't like him but didn't hate him either. Besides, I reasoned, if this was more than an accident, he could give me information that might impress the clown. Might give me a raise...might even...my thoughts drifted to *Ink Spot.*

Chen interrupted my daydream. "So, we're good?" He extended his hand.

"Yeah, we're good." His grip felt strong and confident and at the same time, warm and familiar like the touch of a close friend. For a split second, I had this wacky thought of how nice it would be to curl up inside that hand and sleep. I felt safe. Uncomfortable and confused by the feeling, I tried to pull back. "I have to report in. So, if I don't see you around, enjoy Seattle." Now, instead of safe, I felt stupid. What a lame thing to say. Enjoy Seattle. Jeez.

He held on for a flash too long, then let go. He didn't say anything else before he turned and stepped back onto the smoldering deck of Shirley Cantrell's home.

I stopped at Dorothy's houseboat on my way up the dock. The tarp and folding table were gone but the Tupperware box balanced on the deck's railing. A hand-lettered sign read, "Fresh cookies, please help yourself." I left the coffee mug on the railing and helped myself to the baked goods. Figured an oatmeal raisin cookie was the closest thing to breakfast I would get this morning.

Except for the lingering smell and hazy smoke of the fire, the dock was bright and inviting. I noticed things I hadn't seen earlier—flowers on every deck, unlocked bicycles propped against railings, kayak paddles, piles of PFDs, flip-flops, and running shoes lined neatly outside doors. Yes, a sweet little community. Good neighbors. I imagined Shirley would be missed.

I'd almost reached the end of the dock when something heavy flew out of nowhere and smacked onto my day pack. I screamed.

"What the fu..." I looked toward the stairs for help, but the two cops who were supposed to be guarding had disappeared. I spun around—flapped my arms—tried to shake the thing off. Tried to wriggle out of my day pack. I managed to reach over my shoulder and grab the thing. My fingers touched flesh. I dug in and pulled.

*Yeowwwwww!* It screeched. Sounded like a rabid alley cat or an angry poltergeist. And it wasn't letting go. With a final jerk, I managed to wrench one shoulder out of my day pack and spin around. I slipped out of the other strap and dropped the pack to the deck.

I stared at the thing. It stared at me. More alien than feline. Wide eyes with pupils so dilated I couldn't tell their color. Almost hairless except for a few tufts of scorched fur. Skin raw, blackened, and bleeding in spots. The creature clung to my pack, claws gripped, frozen in place. This, I knew, was Shirley's cat. Alive, and for sure, it had gone through hell. I reached out and slowly extended one hand.

"Kitty?"

It leaped from the day pack to my chest, buried its claws in my denim jacket and held on. I pressed my hand against its back for support.

So, there we were, a crazed cat and a shocked red-head, embracing on an empty dock, in smoke-hazed sunlight, on a damp Seattle morning.

# 6

I carried the critter the three blocks to my car, kicked Roger's door open and lowered the cat to the tangle of clothes, fast-food wrappers, and papers cluttering the backseat. That animal seemed to know it was safe. Or, maybe it was too exhausted to care. I watched it for a moment. It sniffed around, found a wrinkled flannel shirt, rounded into a ball, coughed, and closed its eyes. Within minutes, the poor thing was fast asleep.

Before smacking the dashboard, I grabbed the ticket from under my wiper, crumpled it into a ball, and tossed it on the passenger's seat. I fished Chen's card from my pocket and programmed his number into my phone. His ringtone? The theme from an old reality TV show. *Bad boys, bad boys. Whatcha gonna do when they come for you?*

The clown hunched over the sink in the break room scrubbing his favorite coffee mug with a Brillo pad. I couldn't see his face but guessed it would be red with exertion. I plopped my day pack on the floor and my butt in a chair. My stomach growled. One oatmeal cookie was

not enough to soak up a night of drinking and not enough
to fill an empty belly. I hoped Broom would hurry up,
admonish me for missing our fifteen minutes of fame,
and let me go home. I watched him work for a couple of
minutes and then offered the one and only housekeeping
tip I knew.

"So, Glen, betcha baking soda gets rid of coffee stains
faster than scrubbing."

"Not coffee stains," he mumbled. "Worse." He
worked a little longer and then filled his cup with soapy
water and left it in the sink to soak. He dried his hands
and pointed to his office.

Although we were the only ones in the building, and
the chance of anyone wandering in was almost non-
existent, he closed the door. He turned to me as he
wiped sweat from his forehead.

"Blue," he said, "*we* have a problem."

After several of Glen's attempts to explain things, I
finally understood what was happening to—or at least
what was planned for—Dock W. Apparently, Elaine
Dupont, a member of the city's most elite, had managed
to buy all except four of the houseboats on the dock.
Mrs. Dupont planned to turn the area into an upscale
playground for the extremely rich. It would come complete with high-end boutiques, elegant waterfront
dining, an art gallery, a jazz bar, and the offices of the
exclusive law firm of Furlow, Furlow, and Wade. Gated
entry and valet parking would make it the perfect alter-
native to Seattle's existing waterfront, where currently
even riffraff like me were allowed to stroll.

"How can she put a commercial enterprise in the middle of those residential docks?" I thought about how peaceful and welcoming the houseboat community had seemed despite the morning's tragedy.

My boss stared at me with a look that seemed to ask, *Are you completely dense*? Taking a deep breath, he tried to explain the situation.

"Sheaffer, people like the Duponts don't worry about building permits. They have busloads of lawyers...and probably..." he paused and chewed on his lower lip for a second, "a few politicians in their pockets." He glared at me. "This is between us. This entire thing is between us. Understood?"

Even though I nodded, I wasn't entirely convinced it could stay "between us." I thought of David Chen. He didn't strike me as the kind of man who would be swayed by politics or money. And he didn't seem like the kind of detective who would settle for an easy explanation.

"Who refused to sell?" Although I had a hunch, I asked anyway.

The clown snatched a sheet of paper from his desk and read down a list. "Number Seven—owner, Geraldine Galloway. Number Three—owner, Dorothy Appleton. Bud Ordwell, Number Nine—owner, and Number Twelve, the one that burned, owner, Shirley Cantrell." He dropped the paper back on his desk.

"So, you're telling me that if the fire was an accident and the dead woman didn't have a beneficiary, then the insurance payout will go to probate and hold up the project, right?"

Broom dug in his pocket for his handkerchief. "Yes. That's what I've been saying all along." He mopped his forehead with what looked to me like a soiled and sweat-soaked rag.

"And, if it wasn't an accident...let's say it was..." I started to say murder but Broom held up his hand.

"It was suicide. Plain and simple. The poor woman was under a lot of pressure to sell her home, and she was most likely depressed." He paced the room a couple more times and then stopped in front of me. "Look, Sheaffer. I feel bad for her, but she's gone. There's no sense in...so you just do your job. Investigate this incident. Dig around. Find some evidence she *really was* depressed. And report to me the minute you get anything. Got it?"

I stood. "Yeah, I got it." I picked up my day pack and started for the door.

"And Sheaffer..." Broom stepped in front of me. "Like I said before, this conversation—all of it. It's just between us. Right?"

I looked at the man who paid my wages. His face was puffy and red—shiny with sweat. His expression twisted with fear and desperation. He no longer reminded me of a clown. Clowns can be funny. This man wasn't funny. He was pathetic. I wanted to tell him where he could shove his incident and his wealthy client. I didn't.

"Sure. On it." I mumbled my words and left.

Broom had been so freaked out that he didn't even mention the fact I'd screwed up our media moment. At first, I was relieved, but by the time he got done pacing, wringing his doughy hands, and pouring out his woes, I almost wished he'd been yelling at me rather than taking me into his confidence. I didn't like the sound of "*we* have a problem," and "*we* need to be discreet," and "*we* need to handle this carefully." On the short walk to Roger, I kept thinking how I'd been hired to fill out forms about petty crime, broken windows, and car-to-garage-door run-ins. But, so far, on this day—and it wasn't even noon—my job description included dealing with a burned body, a hard-assed cop, a client who held the company hostage, possible homicide, possible suicide, and a partially toasted feline. Not what I signed up for.

When I reached the car, I kicked the door open and leaned over the seat to check on the cat. It was still alive and still asleep on my crumpled shirt. I wasn't too worried that I didn't have a plan for it—at the moment I had more stressful issues than what to do with a homeless, hairless cat. Like, for example, where to find my next job.

I parked in the marina lot and took a couple of minutes to dump everything out of my day pack onto Roger's front seat. Then I scooped up the cat, shirt and all, and stuffed it into the pack. The poor critter opened its eyes, yawned, and nestled back down into the warm cocoon. I slipped into my day pack and ambled down my dock to *Ink Spot*.

I was in the middle of debating whether I should give a two-week notice or simply walk out when I saw Willie, the marina manager, snap a padlock through links of a heavy chain. The chain looped through an iron cleat on the dock and around the headsail on my boat, making it impossible for me to sail away, or to even motor out of the slip.

"Willie! What the hell are you doing?" Forgetting about the cat, I jogged the rest of the length of the dock.

Willie was about seventy, gray-haired, skinny, and stooped over. He'd been managing the marina with a laissez-faire attitude for the past fifty years. He stood, pulled his baseball cap off and scratched his head.

"I'm sorry, Blue," he said. "You know, if it was up to me..." He replaced the cap, looked down at the dock and shuffled his feet.

"But why? You know I'll get the money. I get paid next week."

Willie cleared his throat and spat into the lake. "Ah yeah, okay. You know, you're three months behind now. The owner says you have to pay up or..."

"Or what?" My body shook. *Ink Spot* was my world. *Ink Spot* was everything. This was *not* happening.

"Ah, Blue. You know if there was anything I could do..." Willie spat again and avoided eye contact. He looked miserable.

I knew it wasn't his fault. He'd let me slide on the rent several times, and he put up with my not-so-discreet parties. He didn't even mention the time my buddies and I rammed a tugboat into the dock in the middle of the night. I was pretty sure he knew who did the damage, but he didn't say a word—he simply made the repairs and let it drop. This action today was, for sure, demanded by the marina owner. Still, I was so upset I couldn't control my temper.

"This is an outrage, Willie. Pure bullshit and you know it!"

He glanced up at me, started to speak, and then stopped cold. His eyes widened, his jaw dropped. "Sweet mother of Jesus!"

Right then, the cat, who'd poked his raw, burned, and blackened head up from my day pack gave a long and terrifying howl. Willie crossed himself and took off at a gallop up the dock.

Clearly, our discussion of late rent and purloined sailboats was over. At least for now. I reached around and patted the wrinkled head.

"Shuuuuuush, little buddy. It's okay. We'll figure it out...we'll be okay."

# 7

Geraldine's eyes flickered from Bud to Dorothy.

"I wish Charlie was here. He'd come up with a plan. He'd know what to do."

"Well, I certainly don't have any ideas." Dorothy refilled Bud's coffee cup. "Those two young policemen never leave the front door. There's no way they're going to let us go in now that it's a..." She stopped—didn't want to say the words, "crime scene" out loud. She flushed a moment and then held the coffeepot up to Geraldine. Geraldine shook her head.

"We have to do something, damn it." Bud's lower lip trembled—he wavered between anger and sadness. "Shirley always said that if anything happened to her, we should get her Christmas tin—her baking was the best thing she could ever leave us. Seems such a damn shame to let it be tossed away." His anger got the best of him, and he slapped his hand on Dorothy's end table. Coffee splashed from his cup onto a lace doily. "Oh, sorry, Dot." He tried to mop the spill with a crumpled tissue.

"Never mind." Dorothy waved it off. "You're right, of course. We need to get it. If they find it, they'll think she was an old stoner who bumped herself off in a stupor. That is, of course, if it even survived the fire."

"Not to mention, we'll probably never get any more brownies like Shirley's." Geraldine whimpered.

For a moment, the three friends sat quietly, barely breathing. Each struggled to devise a plan to save Shirley's last gift. Outside, in the real world, dinghy motors rumbled, construction workers called to each other, and sirens screamed from the freeway. In the stillness of Dorothy's houseboat, the only sound came from the swish of the plastic tail and the click of the rotating eyes on her Felix-the-Cat clock.

Geraldine's thoughts were multicolored, almost psychedelic. Sometimes she was aware that her train of thought was slowly derailing. Other times she delighted in the strange ways notions flicked in and out. Luckily, she still had her art. It was Shirley who had first encouraged her to paint and Shirley who, after all these years, continued to make monthly trips to the craft store for supplies. Geraldine's lower lip trembled. She might have wept, but she noticed a butterfly resting on the windowsill and her thoughts turned to the color orange.

Dorothy closed her eyes and took in a slow, deep breath. Shirley had been her best friend, her first college roommate, the one who had stayed by her side and had kept her from self-destructing when her husband and two young sons were killed in the car wreck. If it hadn't been for Shirley, Dorothy would have been carried out in a black body bag decades ago. Now, Shirley— or at least her reputation—needed protecting. Dorothy exhaled and opened her eyes. She glanced over at Bud.

Bud scrunched his brow into deep furrows. He was out of his comfort zone. He was a follower—a steady, reliable follower. The planning and leading of shenanigans had been Shirley's domain. Their friend Charlie, with his accountant's brain and his calm demeanor, revised the plans so they didn't all end up in jail—or worse. Shirley had organized sit-ins and marches and what she called "acts of civic consciousness."

Graduation didn't slow her down; she spent her life working for women's rights, civil rights, the rights of animals, and anything to do with saving the Earth. Bud had been in awe of, and secretly in love with, Shirley for half a century, but she didn't notice. If she did, she never let on. The one time he'd broached the subject she said that her heart had been broken once and once was more than enough. That was the end of it. Still, after all this time, he continued to cherish her. Now, he felt, it was up to him to champion her final cause.

Finally, he snapped his fingers. "I've got it!" he said.

Bud laid out his plan for the ladies. When he finished, they howled with laughter. Geraldine clapped her hands and did a little dance around the sofa. Dorothy grabbed Bud and gave him a tight squeeze.

"You are a genius," she said. "This is the kind of thing Shirley would think up."

Bud beamed. It was the highest compliment he could ever remember.

Dorothy made turkey sandwiches. Geraldine heated homemade clam chowder and poured it into two covered plastic bowls. Bud went back to his houseboat and collected a couple of bottles of O'Doul's Non-Alcoholic Beer.

When everything was ready, Dorothy loaded the food and drink into a large picnic basket, Bud carried the folding table, and Geraldine dragged two folding chairs. It was slow going as the three friends made their way down the dock to the two police officers standing guard in front of the crime scene.

"Check it out," one nudged his partner. "Gramps and two grannies heading this way."

"What are they carrying?" The other asked.

"Yoo-hoo! Mr. Policemen!" Geraldine called out, her voice a high-pitched trill.

The cops grinned. "Here, let me help you with that." The youngest rushed down the dock and took the chairs from her. "Are you folks planning a picnic?"

"No, officer," Bud said. "We're bringing you fellows lunch."

"Our friend lived here," Dorothy glanced at the burned houseboat. "We want to thank you for protecting it from looters and other hoodlums."

The officers looked at each other and shrugged. They'd been standing on the dock all morning with nothing more than coffee and a bag of donuts. They could eat and guard at the same time. Besides, no one had even walked by since that detective left, and that had been at least three hours ago. Lunch sounded good.

They helped Bud set up the table and then watched, amused, as Dorothy and Geraldine covered it with an embroidered cloth, set plates and silverware out, and then arranged soup, sandwiches, and drinks.

"Dig in, officers." Bud gestured to the table.

"You folks going to eat?" One cop asked, taking a seat.

"No, dear," Geraldine said. "We're going to my place. It's the light blue one." She pointed to a houseboat at the end of the dock. "We'll come back and get the table and the rest of it in a little while." With that, the two ladies linked arms and strolled down the dock. Bud trailed behind them.

The officers watched for a moment, then turned to their lunch. "Nice people," one said. "Remind me of my grandparents."

"Yeah. Friendly folks," his partner added.

They were five minutes into their lunch when they heard the commotion.

"Help! Help!" Bud came stumbling back up the dock waving his arms. "I think she's having a heart attack or stroke or something. Help!"

The cops bolted out of their seats, dashed past Bud, and raced down the dock toward the senior women. One radioed for an EMT backup. Dorothy wailed at the top of her lungs as she pointed to Geraldine, who lay flat on her back, flopping like a fish.

Deciding she'd be better off with her friends than alone in her own home, the EMTs stretched Geraldine out on Dorothy's sofa and told her to rest for a while. Apparently, she was fine, probably just exhaustion or stress from the fire and the death of her neighbor. When the medics left, Dorothy brewed a pot of tea. The policemen carried the table and chairs back to her house. Bud followed with the picnic basket.

The officers declined cups of tea, thanked the ladies for the soup and sandwiches, and wished Geraldine a speedy recovery. They shook Bud's hand and left to resume guard duty in front of Shirley's houseboat.

The three friends drank tea in silence. They barely breathed for a full twenty minutes. Finally, Dorothy tiptoed to the window and peeked around her lace curtain. The dock was empty. She turned and glanced down at the picnic basket by Bud's chair.

"Did you get it?" she said.

Bud bent down, opened the basket and with a grand flourish, removed a dented tin box decorated with a Currier and Ives Christmas scene. The ladies gasped, and then they clapped.

# 8

The cat picked through the disarray in my salon while I rummaged in the galley cupboards for something that resembled feline food. Given that the last time I went grocery shopping was about the last time I'd done laundry, the choices were slim. I could maybe grind up some stale pretzels. Maybe that would resemble kibble. Or, I wondered, do cats like olives? I read the label and learned that the jar was three years out of date and contained a high level of salt. Cats like salt, right? Finally, in the far back of the bottom shelf, right behind the flare gun, I discovered two cans of tuna packed in oil. Perfect. Food for the cat. Food for me.

I dumped one can onto a dish and set it on the floor under the table. I placed a bowl of water next to the tuna. Lack of fur didn't hamper that cat's appetite. It lit into the fish like it had never eaten before. I watched it for a minute, wondered what color its fur would be once it grew back in—if it grew back in. From my vantage point, I could tell it was a Tom. All boy. I wondered what I was going to do with him. No-kill shelter?

Craigslist? Who would take a traumatized, furless, scary-sounding cat?

At the insistence of my grumbling stomach, I opened the second can of fish, dumped it into a bowl, and added a squirt of stone-ground mustard. That, with some sea salt and cayenne pepper, made lunch.

I took the tuna and a warm beer up to the cockpit. My refrigerator had stopped working a couple of weeks back, not a serious problem, but an expensive one and I didn't have the cash to make the repair. At the time I'd laughed it off, made some comment about the health value of warm beer and the importance of learning to live without refrigeration, because if something breaks on the ocean, well...there are no repair shops at sea. Now, sitting on a stack of cracked and moldy cushions, eating a dish of mustard-flavored tuna fish, it didn't seem so funny. Nothing seemed funny.

It wasn't the warm beer that got to me—it was everything that had happened that morning. I glanced past the lifelines to the chain that held my boat captive. I had about eighteen dollars in cash and maybe another three or four in change scattered under cushions or hiding in jars. Payday was a week away, and even if I handed my entire check to Willie, it wouldn't be enough to buy *Ink Spot's* freedom. There was no way I could quit my job now, no matter how shitty it felt to me.

I thought about my meeting with the clown. I'd been stuck in that stupid chair for forty-five minutes. He paced the entire time—his sweat soaking through his shirt. He knew that what he wanted me to do was wrong, but he was too freaked about losing his business to care.

"She wants this cleared up fast," he'd said. "She's got a team of architects and contractors lined up. She's got millions riding on her project and doesn't want it delayed."

The whole thing made me sick, yet there wasn't a lot I could do at this point. At least, I didn't think there was anything I could do. I had to stay with the job long enough to get *Ink Spot* out of hock. Then, maybe, I'd forget about making repairs to the generator, forget about buying a new headsail. Get real comfortable with warm beer. Sell Roger, use the money for fuel and take off down the coast. Get to Mexico no matter what. I could probably pick up a waitressing gig in a gringo bar and save money for boat repairs there. At least I'd be out of the rain. At least I'd be free. First, however, I had to prove that Shirley Cantrell had committed suicide— whether she had or hadn't.

The roar of a seaplane circling above the city pulled my thoughts back to the cockpit. I gathered up the empty bottle and bowl, went below, and dropped them into the sink. The cat had disappeared. Probably found some dark corner to hide in. I hoped he felt safe.

About halfway up the dock, I remembered that the cat didn't have a litter box. On the way back to *Ink Spot* I returned a wave from a fellow boater and bantered with another who joked and called out, "Hey, Blue! Wanna borrow my bolt cutters?"

Much as I wanted to sail away, and as bummed as I was at the time, I still enjoyed the comradery and friendship of the liveaboards in this funky mid-city marina. I grinned and gave a cheerful one-fingered salute to my neighbor. He took it in the spirit offered.

When I reached my boat, I searched for something that would serve as litter and a potty-box. For litter, I settled on dried dirt from a flowerpot. The plant had long since died from neglect. I dumped it into a make-shift litter pan—the bottom half of the empty pizza box. I left the dirt-filled container on the floor in the head. The cat would figure it out.

My plan for the rest of the day was to interview Shirley's neighbors to see if any of them had ideas about what might have caused the fire. I figured the police, the fire investigator, and David Chen were all way ahead of me on this, but at least I'd be on the clock.

As I walked down Dock W toward the burned house-boat, I noticed two cops guarding the crime scene. I didn't know them, but I stopped and chatted for a few minutes, explained my role, and let them know that I'd be snooping around. I told them to give David Chen a call if they want-ed to verify my story. If anything, they seemed happy for the contact. Except for a few minutes of excitement—an older woman had fallen on the dock and required oxy-gen—their day had been quiet and boring. I nodded to the crumpled donut-shop bag on Shirley's deck and promised to bring a refill on my next trip.

I moved on down the dock, taking in the surroundings until the sharp odor of cigarette smoke caught my atten-tion. A woman leaned on the doorway of a weatherworn structure. Faded sea-green paint peeled from the build-ing's walls and deck-planters sat empty save for muddy pools left by the morning rain. Mid-afternoon and the woman was still dressed in a pink, coffee-stained bathrobe. Her face reminded me of a "Before" photo in a wrinkle cream ad. She held a freshly lit smoke in one hand and a tall glass of watery-looking orange juice in the other. She called out to me, and from the slur of her words, I guessed it wasn't water diluting the juice.

"You with the cops? Cuz I already told my story to those pigs."

"No," I said as I stepped to her railing. "No, I'm an insurance investigator. Nothing heavy. Just getting some, you know, facts for a report." I glanced around. Her deck offered a panoramic view of Lake Union, the downtown skyline, and the iconic Space Needle. "Nice view you've got here."

She coughed. Took a drag, blew smoke, and then gulped her drink. "Yeah. It's okay, but I'm sick of this stinking city. Got free rent until the first of the year and then I'm going back to Montana. That's God's country."

"Free rent, eh? That's cool. Wish I could score something like that." I've learned the best way to deal with heavy drinkers is to be light, casual, avoid any complexities. And, get away as fast as possible.

"Only free because that idiot ex of mine sold this dump to that rich bitch. It was supposed to be my retirement investment, but he cheated me outta it. Asshole." Another cough.

I tried to look sympathetic.

"Say, you want a screwdriver?" She held up her glass.

I sighed. "Wish I could, but I gotta write this stupid report today. Sounds good, though."

"Suit yourself." She shrugged and took another gulp.

"So, you know that houseboat that burned down this morning? Did you know the woman who lived there?"

She dropped the cigarette into a coffee can filled with tea-colored water and dozens of soaked butts. It hissed and disappeared. She fished a pack from her bathrobe pocket and lit another. "Yeah, I seen her around. Druggie." She took a long pull on the smoke and gazed skyward as she exhaled.

"Druggie?"

"Yeah. Those boys, the ones with their pants down their butts—always goin' in and outta there. Drugs. That old broad was probably dealing. Opioids is my guess— probably told her doc she was in pain." She hesitated, seemed to be thinking. "A course, you can't blame her. Damn government makes it hard for old people to sur- vive. Gotta do whatcha gotta do." She paused, then added, "That's why I'm going to Montana, first chance I get."

"Did the old woman ever seem depressed?" I took a step backward, started my exit strategy.

She leaned forward, giving me a whiff of stale ciga- rettes and a glimpse of way more withered flesh than I ever wanted to see.

"She wasn't depressed. She was pissed off. Wanted us to organize—resist the sale of the dock. I think it was the drugs talking." She straightened and finished off the rest of her drink. "Well, lookie that. Time for me to whip up some more Vitamin C. Sure I can't interest you in taking a little break?"

"No, thanks, but um...one more thing. Do you think the fire was an accident?"

She bent down and motioned for me to step closer. Not something I actually wanted to do but...

"I think those boys are a gang. I think they got greedy. Didn't want to pay for their drugs no more so they went in there, bumped the old gal off. Probably trashed the place and set it on fire. Probably got gang points for it. That's what I think." She swayed a bit when she stood. "This place is going into the toilet. That's why I'm going to Montana."

Then, without another word, she dropped her smoke into the coffee can, turned, and disappeared behind the chipped and peeling door of her soon-to-be vacated houseboat.

I stood in front of her deck for a moment. She disgusted me—this woman drowning in a blend of fruit juice and booze. She'd probably spent most of her life hiding at the bottom of a bottle. At the same time, I felt sad. Sometimes life seems too scary to face without a little help. I knew that—I'd done some hiding in my three decades. I took a breath to clear my thoughts— this wasn't the time for regrets or self-reflection. That time would come—but it wasn't now. I trucked on down the dock.

I'd been charmed by the look and feel of the community during my first visit, but now I noticed that while most of the houseboats were well-kept and tidy on the outside, they appeared empty. Only a handful had a lived-in look and I could imagine that maybe, like the boozy juice woman's ex, the former owners didn't want to join Shirley's fight against Elaine Dupont's lawyers. Maybe they'd simply taken the payout and left. Pity.

I walked until I reached the lake and spent a couple of minutes admiring the water, the cityscape, and the baby-blue houseboat at the dock's end. The small building could use a coat of paint and the flower beds needed weeding, yet despite its slightly shabby appearance, the modest houseboat offered a welcoming feeling. It looked like the kind of place where you could sit on the deck with a glass of lemonade and watch the world go by, comfortable in the knowledge you'd be safe and secure when you went inside and settled for the night. I'd felt that way on the deck of *Ink Spot* many times. But lately, with money worries and mounting repairs, even my boat failed to offer the comforts of home. *Shit, Blue.* I admonished myself. *What is your problem today? Get a grip, girl, and get on with it.* I turned and headed back up the dock.

A few yards away a short, round woman swept dust and dry bird droppings into the water. I stopped and introduced myself. She leaned on her broom and took a break from her work.

"Is this your home?" I nodded to the large houseboat behind her.

"No," she said. "I used to work here as a housekeeper until the owners sold it to Mrs. Dupont and moved to Hawaii. Mrs. Dupont kept me on, though. She wants to keep it clean so some lawyers can move in when she takes over." The woman glanced over her shoulder at the imposing structure. It was the most expensive appearing and the most elegant property on the dock. "I have family in Mexico and I need to send them money.

Maybe the lawyers will need a housekeeper for the office. So, I stay."

I asked if she knew Shirley, if she thought Shirley was depressed, and if she thought the fire was an accident. The woman seemed to consider my questions for a moment and then she pushed a bit of dirt across the dock.

"I talk with her sometimes. She was mad," she said. "She told everybody to fight for their home, but nobody did. Except for her and her friends, everybody else took the money." The woman sighed and brushed at the dock.

"Are you sure she was angry? Are you sure she wasn't depressed?" I didn't like saying those words—hadn't liked hearing them, but I'd decided to give it my best shot—give the clown a real report.

The woman shook her head. "No. I know for sure. She was mad. But..." She stopped sweeping and looked at me. "I tell you this. She was sad in her heart. Broken heart."

"Because she had to sell her house?" I said.

"No. She was mad about the house. She was sad in her heart about love." The woman sighed, reached up and touched the cross hanging from a silver chain around her neck. "Some things I know." With that, she turned from me and resumed her sweeping. No doubt about it, our discussion had come to an end.

I squinted toward the sun—still enough time to chat with a couple more residents if I could find them. My stomach made a low grumbling sound—so much for the staying power of tuna.

As I walked toward the head of the dock, I decided to pop over to my friend Lilly's studio later—she cooks all the time. Her food is weird, new-agey, and experimental, and she is always happy to share. Plus, she has a habit of picking up and re-homing stray critters. I knew I could score real kibble and some proper litter from her. And I knew she'd have advice on what to do with my furless roommate. Maybe she'd even find a new home for him.

I was deep into rehearsing the "oh you will love this kitty" speech when five kids in their late teens, maybe early twenties, piled out of a squat brown houseboat at the head of the dock. They jostled and dissed each other in the joking manner of close friends. From their denim pants held up with nothing but luck, backward ball caps, T-shirts, and skateboards tucked under their arms, I guessed this was "the gang" the OJ woman had mentioned. One of them spotted me and catcalled.

"Yo, mama! You too hot!" He slammed his skateboard to the dock, jumped on, and raced toward me, the wheels clack, clack, clacking at each board edge. He stopped a foot away, hopped off, and expertly flipped his board up and into his hand. I guessed he was the leader.

"Wow," I said, "I am totally impressed. You've got your moves down."

His face flushed and he worked hard to maintain his too cool expression. I could tell he was both pleased and embarrassed. "What you doin' in our hood, mama?"

His friends gathered around us. They stood a little too close for my comfort, but I knew these were only kids filling in time. I wished I could do something impressive for them, like flaunt a badge or even a business card. Lacking both, I flashed the brightest smile I could and winked at the leader. His buddies laughed.

"You okay, girl," he said. Then he tilted his head to one side and asked, "Whatcha need? Everybody need somethin'."

"Well, I need to know why that houseboat burned down," I said.

"You with the cops?" A boy wearing a torn Che Guevara T-shirt snarled at me. "'Cause we already told the cops. We got nothin' to do with that."

"Right," another chimed in. "Everybody think we bump off ol' ladies for drug money. But that ain't true."

"No way," I rocked back and forth and stuck my thumbs in my back pockets—tried to look casual. "I am for sure—definitely—not with the cops. Just investigating for her insurance company. For Shirley. The old lady who lived there. Did you guys know her?"

They paused a minute and looked at each other. Tensed. Then they zeroed in on me "You sure you're not with the cops?" The leader took a step closer.

"Sure." I nodded—first serious then flirty. "I might have to, you know...once in a while, to get out of a ticket. But I'm positively not *with* the cops." I tilted my head and tried to give one of those "know what I'm sayin?" looks.

"She okay." The kid glanced at his buddies. He turned back to me.

"Like he say, no way we bump off Shirley for drug money. It the opposite. Old Shirl-girl, she buy weed from us. Even it be legal for, like forever, she say she rather support the locals than buy from the pot shops and pay taxes to the man." He looked a little wistful for a moment. "Yeah, she was okay."

"So," I ventured, "maybe she was smoking weed in bed and fell asleep and dropped—"

"Hell no," Che-boy said. He shook his head emphatically. "She always be after us to quit smoking. Said it would stunt our growth. Shrink our peckers." All five snickered at that.

"Shirley said that?"

The skateboarder nodded. "Shirley hated smokers. She hated rich people, she hated anyone who hurt animals, and she hated politicians. Ol' Shirl-girl, she liked us. Bought weed from us and then cooked it up in a batch of brownies and she always give us a bunch of 'em. She say she was makin' chocolate-covered Mary Jane." He sighed.

"I miss dat ol' girl," Che added. The others nodded in agreement. The leader shrugged.

"Say, mama. You wanna come to our pad? Do some fine, fine stuff? Wipe that serious edge off your pretty face?"

"Gotta get back to work." I looked at their young faces. Boys. Just boys, passing the time. "Rain check?"

Over the clack, clack, clack of skateboard wheels on wooden slats I heard a snatch of conversation from my new buddies.

"She not so bad for an old chick."

I sighed and started up the dock steps. *So, it's come to this. Old chick.*

# 9

I parked Roger in the dirt lot next to a huge corrugated eggplant-colored building that served as the home and studio of Lilly Sugathum. In reality, the building was a Quonset hut painted deep plum. The front door sported a coat of lime green, the back glowed flamingo pink. In the right light, you'd swear it was a large bruised vegetable lying on a bed of brown rice.

Lilly is my best friend. We met at the Northwest Folklife Festival years ago, and even though we seem to be at opposite ends of some strange spectrum, we're as close as twin sisters. We know each other's strengths and sorrows and secrets. We know how to coax a smile when times are tough and how to play together. Close as we are, I can never predict what she'll come up with next. I guess I shouldn't be surprised. Lilly comes from a long line of performance artists and from what I can tell, they are all as trippy as her.

Take her Uncle Marv, for example. He erected the Quonset hut when a bad case of gout forced him to quit traveling with the Barnum and Bailey Circus. Uncle Marv loved animals, and he had lots of them—dogs, roosters, rabbits, monkeys, even a billy goat. They all lived together in his galvanized-steel home. Whenever one of his pets died, he had it stuffed, encased in concrete, painted in lifelike colors and mounted on the curved roof of the structure. When Marv passed away, he left the hut to Lilly on the condition that his beloved pets remain in place. I looked up and gave a quick salute to the small zoo that oversaw the otherwise posh neighborhood of Magnolia.

When I pushed the front door open, a shower of sparkling red-and-yellow glitter rained down on me. See what I mean about Lilly?

I brushed at my clothes and shook my head. Glitter swirled from my hair. Slipping out of my deck shoes, I followed the sound of a slow drumbeat. I knew better than to knock or call out, as Lilly could be in the middle of almost anything. She offered a variety of classes in her studio—classes like Breathing for Beginners, Dance against Depression, and Harmonics with House Plants.

She'd tried, many times, to enroll me in one of her classes—usually something for relaxation, or clarity, or inner calm—but honestly, much as I love her, it was all too woo-woo for me. I'd rather sit on the bow of *Ink Spot* with my feet propped on the lifelines and a cold beer in my hand. That's *my way* to inner calm.

Lilly sat cross-legged in the middle of the polished wood floor with her eyes closed and her head thrown back. She beat on an antique Native American drum with something that looked like a carved glass penis. I didn't ask. She'd sprinkled crushed eggshells in a circle—I tiptoed in and squatted in front of her.

"Lil?"

Without opening her eyes or missing a beat, she held up her open palm as a signal that this might take a while. I yawned, stretched out on my back, and gazed at the ceiling. A couple of years earlier Lilly had charmed me into helping her paint a rainbow that stretched the full length of the building. I slid along its pastel arch for a moment, then closed my eyes and let my breathing slow to match the steady thump, thump, thump of crystal phallus on stretched skin. "Blue? Blue, baby?" Lilly stood next to me—her bare feet close enough for me to smell the melon scent of her body lotion. "Get up, my sleepy friend. Let me make you a snack."

I tried a warm, gluten-free, goat cheese and organic pesto scone. It looked sketchy, sort of greenish and lumpy but it smelled delicious. Lilly crumbled tea leaves into a ceramic pot. She mumbled to herself, dropped a bunch of leaves on the floor, and almost broke a cup when she clinked it on the side of her counter. My friend rarely moved more than a point above trance on the agitation scale, so I wondered what caused this unusual mood.

I glanced around the space she called her "nourish-ment nest." Same selection of garage sale pots and pans hanging from a tree branch. Same troop of paper-mache fairies dancing at the ends of curling ribbons. Same jumble of jars filled with herbs, spices, dried fruit, and rose hips. Purple marker ink and childlike printing la-beled the contents. In any other collection like this, you might expect to find jars filled with eye-of-newt or snout of salamander. But Lilly is a vegetarian.

Although everything seemed familiar, I knew something was missing. It took a moment and then I remembered. "Where are your students, Lil? I thought you had a new class starting today."

Lilly turned, put her hands on her hips and pouted. "I did," she said. "Twirling for Twins. I had two sets, and it would have been divine. But they had to cancel because they were carpooling and couldn't get over the I-90 bridge. Because of the accident."

"Accident?" I bit into something gooey and examined the scone more carefully. Now, don't get me wrong, I do like pesto. Especially with pasta. But there was something about the snotty green goo oozing over a clump of gray seeds that reminded me of an episode involving copious amounts of lime-flavored schnapps and a bucket of raw oysters. I set the scone on my plate.

Lilly didn't seem to notice. She handed me a cup of tea—no doubt something organic, no doubt something good for me—something calming or cleansing. She pursed her lips and gazed at one of the fairies spinning slowly overhead. "In truth, there are no accidents. Only Universal Movements that we don't understand. Everything has a purpose. No accidents. Besides, we're in a blue moon, so there's a whole lot more weird stuff to come."

The moon comment made no sense to me so I ignored it and focused on the non-accident. "But they had to close the bridge, right? Did cars collide in...um...a movement?"

Lilly shook her head. Tiny bells woven into her blond dreadlocks tinkled. Bits of glitter fell onto the plate of scones. She took a deep breath and launched into a breathless description.

"No, it wasn't about cars. They were repairing the bridge and there was still one lane open, but then they found a skeleton in one of the columns, and the police made them shut the whole bridge down." She paused for a breath and a sip of her tea. She frowned and set the cup on the table. "Needs honey," she said.

I perked up. A skeleton? In the I-90 bridge?

Lilly stood, turned her back to me and searched a cupboard for honey. I took the opportunity to wrap my scone in a paper napkin and slide it into my day pack. It would return to the earth by way of the marina garbage bin.

"Lil? You were telling me about the skeleton?"

She found the honey and returned to the table. "Yes, it was awful because like I said they were fixing the bridge and I think they have to replace all the old columns or something like that and when they broke open one of the columns a leg bone fell out." She shuddered. "Awful." She glanced at my empty plate and smiled wide. "More?"

"No. It was yummy, but I'm stuffed." I lied and rubbed my stomach.

"Okay. I can send some home with you if you want," she said. "Remind me before you go." She selected a scone from the platter, broke it in two, slathered it with honey, and plowed into the pastry. A stringy piece of vegetation fell from the scone and dangled from the ring in her lower lip.

I winced and waited.

"Mmmm," she murmured. "These turned out way better than I expected."

I tried to steer her back on track. "So, what about the leg bone and the bridge? What else did you hear?"

"Well, they had to stop work on the bridge, and the police blocked traffic, and I guess they have to reinforce the bridge or something before they can take the whole column down. The bones have been there for decades, and they think it will take a whole week before they can get that poor person out of his, or her, cement grave." She sniffled and wiped a tear.

I thought about the critters bolted to the roof above us, started to mention them, but decided it was best to let that one go. I reached over and touched her arm. "I'm sure it was an accident, Lilly. Probably happened fast. Probably no suffering." I changed the subject. "Hey, I've got almost twenty bucks. Why don't we order a pizza? My treat."

Lilly narrowed her eyes for a second. "I thought you were stuffed," she said. Then, true to her nature, she brightened, nodded, stood, twirled around twice—bells tinkling, glitter flying—and flounced off to find the number for *Mamma Zucchini's Organic Pizza Delivery*.

Over Mamma Zucchini's house special—yak cheese topped with seaweed and cucumber slices—I shared the events of my day with Lilly. I told her about the sexy paddleboard instructor with the spider tattoo. Described the destroyed houseboat while leaving out the part about Shirley's charred body and the long black bag. She laughed when I mentioned the senior lady in her yellow shower cap and her friend in red plaid boots.

I worried out loud about my dilemma with work and ever so casually, mentioned the somber detective with his slight limp and warm hands.

Lilly would make a wonderful therapist. She listened, as always, with her full attention. She only took a bite when I paused to eat. She giggled when I told her about the "old chick" comment and took several moments to reflect on the information about Elaine Dupont and her mega-expensive dock project.

"Why would a rich woman like Elaine Dupont hire a dippy little agency like City Wide to insure her project? She could have Lloyd's of London if she wanted."

I shrugged. "I dunno. I wondered about that too."

"Hmmm..." Lilly twirled a dreadlock with one finger. "I bet she picked old Glen Broom because he's such a pushover. She can manipulate him any way she wants without bringing in her lawyers or even much of her money. I bet she dumps him when it's time to insure the new project. Bet she goes with a big company when there are real bucks involved."

I thought about her comment. From what I knew, Elaine Dupont's business pretty much kept City Wide afloat and without that account, Broom would probably go under. Then, no matter what I did around this incident—around Shirley's case—I'd lose my job. And if it happened before I got *Ink Spot* out of hock, I'd be screwed. The whole thing was a lose-lose gig for me. I whined about it for a while. Lilly listened. Finally, she decided that the best thing for us would be a bottle of homemade pineapple wine and a tarot reading.

I do love Lilly—still, sometimes I have to draw a line. I said no to the yellow wine and stepped outside to collect the secret bottle of Jack Daniel's I kept hidden under the spare tire in Roger.

I sunk onto a squishy bean bag in Lilly's sleeping loft, sipped whiskey, and listened to her interpretation of knights and queens and wands until we were both sleepy enough to call it a day.

Lilly pushed her spare futon next to a window for me. From my vantage point, I could watch the big old moon travel slow across the sky. I thought about the hundreds of times I've watched that journey from the deck of my boat, and I vowed that *Ink Spot* and I would sail under many more full moons together, no matter what happened with my job. Somehow, we'd be free. As I stared at the moon, I remembered the conversation Lilly and I had shared earlier.

"Lil? You awake?" I whispered.

"Uh huh," she said. Her voice was soft and low, and I could tell she was about to drift off.

"What did you mean by 'we're in a blue moon and there's more weird stuff to come'?"

"Oh that," she mumbled. "When there are two full moons in one month it's a blue moon month. And you know how strange things get when there's a regular full moon? Well, double the insanity during a blue moon. It gets very, very intense." She rolled over and snuggled deeper into her covers. "But don't worry," she added. "You and me, we can figure it out."

"Thanks, sweetie," I said, though I knew she was already dreaming.

The moon continued to climb, and I let my thoughts drift without course or rudder until they bumped into the burned and freaked-out cat. Cat! I jolted alert. I forgot to tell Lil about the cat. Damn it. I sighed. Oh well...tomorrow. I pulled the blanket over my head, shut out the crazy moon, and let my old buddy Jack lull me to sleep.

# 10

David Chen could feel the elderly woman watching him crab up the dock. This morning his leg hurt more than usual and he knew his limp was more pronounced than it had been the day before. His pain came from an old wound—a battle scar—something he didn't like talking about and he hoped she wouldn't ask about it.

"You hoo, oh, Mr. Detective." She waved to him, then covered her mouth to hide a giggle. A flowing Hawaiian dress draped her short, soft body and a chiffon scarf puffed around her neck. Loose curls matched the pale lavender of her muumuu. "Come have breakfast with us. And..." She paused a moment and scowled, as if maybe slightly confused. Then she brightened. "And we remembered something we want to tell you. Come on in." Her smile wide, she held both arms out in a welcoming gesture.

Chen hesitated. He wanted to decline her invitation because he'd planned to start his interviews at one end of the dock and methodically work his way back to the starting point. She called to him from the deck of a pink houseboat in the middle of the dock. Besides, he'd already interviewed her friend, the owner of the pink houseboat, along with the elderly gentleman who seemed to round out their troop of aging Musketeers. Still, he'd been in the field long enough to know that sometimes second interviews could be helpful. Sometimes, suspects tried to correct what they'd said initially when they were frightened or confused. Their cover-ups could yield more clues than they knew. Other times, innocent bystanders really did remember important information after they'd had time to process what they'd seen or heard. He offered a quick wave and detoured toward the lady with the lavender hair.

He passed on their offer of food partly because he rarely ate much in the morning and partly because he couldn't imagine spaghetti for breakfast, but he sat politely at the table and sipped a cup of coffee while the three friends tilled their way through mounds of noodles slathered in thick, dark tomato sauce. They used chopsticks instead of forks, which made for a messy meal. He found their food selection less puzzling than their silly antics and continuous twittering. The fellow, Bud, tried and failed to spear a meatball with a single stick. The misshapen lump of meat dropped from the plate, rolled across the table, and plopped onto the floor splatting sauce on a yellow-flowered rug. This sent the three seniors into fits of uncontrollable giggles. Coffee snorted from noses; breath caught in gulps. Chen made a mental note to review the early symptoms of dementia and to look into Washington's social services for the elderly.

Finally, the four moved from the table to Dorothy's cozy living room. The two women shared a love seat.

Bud gingerly lowered himself into a rocker and Chen settled into a wingback chair upholstered in worn maroon velvet.

"So," he pulled a notebook from his pocket. "You have something more to share? His comment sobered them. Three gray heads nodded in unison. "Well?"

Bud cleared his throat.

"Well, you see detective, sir, the thing is, we were so upset, you know. Because of Shirley...well, we didn't think..." He coughed.

"I understand," Chen said. "It's all right. Tell me now."

Dorothy reached down and pulled a newspaper from a basket of magazines and catalogs.

"There," she said. She pointed to a photo on the front page. "You asked us if we saw anything unusual on the dock, or anyone going into Shirley's house the day..." She swallowed.

"Go on," Chen said. He reached for the newspaper.

"Well, he was there that morning—we didn't remember when you first asked us. But Larry, he came calling."

Chen studied the color photo on the front page for a moment. A tall, polished man addressed a group of reporters, his expression one of deep professional concern. He stood before the thicket of scaffolding that supported the now closed I-90 bridge. A smaller, black-and-white photo zeroed in on a gaping hole in a crumbling cement column.

The detective handed the paper back to Dorothy. He wrote ALZ (?) in his notebook and then tucked it in his pocket. He leaned forward and looked at each of them, then focused on Geraldine.

"Do you mean to tell me that one of Seattle's port commissioners visited your neighbor, Shirley, the day she died?"

Geraldine nodded solemnly. "Yes. He's Shirley's beau. He came back to her. I always knew he would."

Chen cleared his throat and stood.

Dorothy pointed one finger at him. "Stop right there, young man," she said. "You may think we are a bunch of old fools but if you care anything about doing your job—and protecting the...the—"

"Public," Bud interjected.

"Yes, the public," Dorothy nodded. "Well, you might want to hear us out." She crossed her arms and glared at the detective.

Chen shifted to hide his discomfort, sat back down and retrieved his notebook.

"Okay," he said, "tell me about Shirley's visitor."

## 11

Lilly and I spent the morning chatting over duck egg omelets and coffee. I filled her in on the cat, and she assembled a care package complete with food, litter, a plastic box, an herbal salve to rub on his cuts and burns, a sandwich bag filled with crunchy treats, and two catnip-stuffed mice. As we hugged goodbye, she promised to visit me and the cat as soon as she rescheduled the classes canceled by the bridge closing.

Broom wasn't in when I stopped by City Wide, so I downloaded the photos of the fire scene to his computer and scratched out a quick note that I was on the job. "Don't worry—got this covered." Then I headed for home.

I could hear the yowling from halfway down the dock. Good. Still alive.

With his wrinkled gray skin, lips stretched thin, and eerie alien eyes, he reminded me of E.T.—the movie version extra-terrestrial. He looked frightened and yet when he saw me, he stopped his caterwauling and rubbed his fur-patched body against my leg.

"Oh, poor thing." I picked him up. He purred. I held him close.

He scarfed a bowl of cat food while I dumped the pizza box and set up a real litter pan. When he finished eating, he disappeared into whatever private place he'd found the day before. Even though I reasoned that he needed quiet and a lot of sleep to heal, his absence left me feeling strangely sad. Sad enough to give myself a short lecture. *Get over it, Blue.*

After I showered, changed clothes, and removed the most recent ticket from Roger's windshield, I drove back to Dock W. I had hoped to talk to the neighbor with the barking dogs but when I arrived the "dog-house" was silent. The boys with their low-slung pants, cigarettes, and skateboards were absent as well. The only neighbors out and about were the ladies who'd offered me cookies and coffee. They waved to me and invited me in for lemonade and treats. *Well, why not?*

We settled in Dorothy's living room with an elderly man, introduced as Bud. I listened to their chatter as I nibbled the corner of a strawberry muffin—definitely an improvement over Lilly's pastry.

"We used to pal around together," Geraldine said. "Me and Bud and Dorothy and Shirley and Charlie. We were best friends." She sighed. "That seems so long ago. And now, with Charlie in that awful old folk's home. And with Shirley—"

Dorothy interrupted her. "Don't start, dear. Charlie doesn't live in an awful old folk's home—it's a lovely facility. And besides, let's remember, we have a visitor."

She turned to me. "You are the second person to come by today to investigate the fire."

I immediately thought of Chen. My breath stopped. I mentally chided myself. *Chill, Blue. You're acting weird.* I exhaled. "Who else was here? When?"

"That detective fellow," Bud chimed in. "Early this morning. We were having breakfast. We could tell that, at first, he thought we were dippy in the head." He twirled one finger at his temple. "But when we told him Shirley's old boyfriend paid a visit, well then we had his ear."

I pushed thoughts of Chen away and focused on the matter at hand. "If you don't mind," I said, "I'd like to hear what you shared with the detective."

They didn't need further encouragement. For the second time that day, with great enthusiasm, they launched into the story of Shirley and her gentleman caller. Dorothy handed me a newspaper. She pointed to a photo of a Seattle port commissioner standing in front of the damaged I-90 bridge.

"That fellow, that's Larry Winslow, Shirley's boyfriend. Well, her former boyfriend."

I squinted at the photo. One of Seattle's most prominent—and wealthy—politicians paired with an old woman who lived in a dilapidated, cluttered houseboat? Highly unlikely. I nodded and tried to hide my skepticism.

"I see," I said.

Bud cleared his throat. "Like I said, that detective fellow, he didn't believe us either. But it's true."

Busted. I felt my cheeks burn.

Dorothy smiled at me and let me off the hook. "It was really quite romantic, the way they met," she said.

"It was during one of Shirley's protests. She was big on social justice, you know. That time she was protesting the capture of an octopus from Puget Sound. The university wanted to study it, to learn about its brain. Shirley thought that was cruel. She said it should be allowed to stay in its natural environment and live a long and happy life, so she chained herself to one of the tanks in the new biology lab."

"We were all there." Geraldine grinned. "And a lot of policemen, too. And Larry. He was the photographer for the school newspaper. I can still remember the look on his face when he first saw Shirley. I could tell right then it was love at first sight." She placed her hand over her heart and sighed.

Bud snorted. "More likely lust at first sight if you want my take."

I raised my eyebrows. "Lust?"

"Yep," he nodded "She was chained spread-eagle against that metal tank. That big octopus was splashing around, and Shirley was soaked to the bone. Those nipples of hers stuck out like two little fingers pointing the way to—"

"Bud! Stop it!" Dorothy glared at her friend.

"Well, it's true," Bud mumbled. He lowered his eyes and stared at his hands.

"So, they—Shirley and Larry—they got together in college?" I asked.

"That's right." Dorothy nodded. "They became a team after that protest. Always together. Even though he was a few years younger than us, we let him tag along. Shirley, she was the leader. She was the one who thought up all the different ways we could save the world. And Larry, he followed her around like a lovesick puppy. Honestly, it was all quite sweet."

"He even changed his major from art to political science to be close to her," Geraldine said.

I swallowed a bit of pastry. "Well, what happened? Did they break up?"

The three friends fell silent. Bud busied himself pouring a second glass of lemonade. Geraldine pulled a thread on her scarf. Dorothy did a close examination of her muffin.

"Well," I repeated, "what happened?"

After a few long moments, Bud broke the silence. "It was at Larry's twenty-first birthday party. He got pretty toasted if you know what I mean." Bud looked at me.

I nodded.

He went on. "Well, he got into a pissing match with one of the port commissioners back then. Said it wasn't cool for a big shot politician to invade a private party."

Dorothy jumped in. "But to be fair, he was only looking for his daughter. He knew she went to that party and I think he was worried about her. She was younger than most of us. Not old enough to drink."

Bud nodded. "True enough. Larry, he wanted to impress Shirley by picking a fight with a politician even if the guy was just being a good father. Larry told the commissioner that his daughter was probably having the time of her life right about then. Probably rolling around in the sand under the new bridge construction with a rock musician, or worse, an English major." Bud chuckled and then continued. "Of course, it wasn't true. We all knew it." He coughed and turned away.

"We all knew that girl was safe because Bud called a cab and he and Charlie helped her get into that cab, paid the fare, and sent her home." Geraldine leaned forward. She shook her finger at Bud. "But he couldn't say anything to the commissioner because he felt up that poor drunk girl."

"A little brush over the top of her sweater," Bud mumbled. "And I was drunk too, you know."

As entertaining as these true confessions were, I was getting a little antsy. "So, about Shirley and Larry?"

Dorothy took over. "The commissioner left about then—I guess to go out to the bridge construction to look for his daughter. Larry went after him. Shirley wanted to stay and party, but she figured Larry might need some help, so she went too. And, well...something happened out there. Something she never talked to us about. The next day, Larry quit school. Up and split. He went back home to the Midwest and enrolled in some fancy law school. He wrote one letter to Shirley the day he left, and that was the end of it. She showed us the letter once, but wouldn't let us read it. That was so many years ago." She stopped, folded her hands on her lap, and looked at me.

"Strange," I said, "did they ever see each other again?"

She shook her head. "No. Never."

"Except for the wedding," Geraldine said.

"Wedding?"

"Oh yes," Dorothy said. "I forgot about the wedding. It was oh...decades later. Larry moved back to Seattle and married a younger woman. By then he'd moved into politics—he hung around with all the right people and married into money. Oh, it was a big society wedding. Talk of the town. All over the newspapers. Well, it was winter, and the bridesmaids wore mink wraps over their dresses. Shirley had a fit over the fur. She organized a protest outside the church. When the wedding party came out, Larry and Shirley locked eyes. They didn't say a word—they just stared at each other for a couple of minutes. Then Shirley handed her protest sign and her jar of fake blood to me and left. We didn't see her for days. We guessed she needed some time alone. After that, she never talked about Larry. Ever."

We sat quietly. Then I remembered Geraldine's earlier comment. I tapped the newspaper photo. "But didn't you say that Larry visited her the other day? The same day as the fire?"

Geraldine nodded. "Yes," she said. "He visited her that day, and the fire was that night, you know," she corrected me.

"Are you sure it was him?"

She nodded more rapidly. "Of course, I'm sure. I made a painting."

The four of us stood in a semicircle in Geraldine's living room. We faced a wall painted a deep teal—at least the thin bits that showed were teal. Most of the wall's surface was hidden by a field of drawings and paintings—watercolors, chalks, pen-and-inks, charcoals, acrylics, and even a few oils. When a slight breeze passed through the screen door, dozens of sheets of white drawing paper fluttered like a meadow teaming with pale, cream-winged butterflies.

"Geraldine," I asked, "are all these yours? Did you do all of them?"

She beamed and nodded. "Every one," she said.

"Geraldine earned a certificate in Visual Arts from the Pratt Fine Arts Center." Dorothy put her arm around Geraldine and gave her friend a hug. "We are all so proud of her."

Geraldine blushed a soft pink.

Bud chimed in. "We don't need to write down anything because our artist here makes pictures of everything she sees." He stepped closer. "Look at this for instance." He pointed to a painting high in the right-hand corner of the wall. Even though the edges of the paper crinkled and the colors had faded, Seattle's skyline, pre-Space Needle, was unmistakable.

"I was a young girl when I made that picture," Geraldine said. "That was before I even heard about the art school."

"Wow." I blew a stream of air from pursed lips. "That is amazing. It should be framed. It should be in some museum—some special collection."

Geraldine's blush turned a deep rose, and she looked at the floor. It was clear she was both embarrassed and proud.

"The older ones are on the top," Bud said. "She starts pinning them up high and then works down. And this is only the first wall—the oldest ones. Wait till you see her new collection."

We moved from room to room, wall to wall, staring at Geraldine's work. I didn't know much about art, but I knew what I liked. The sketches and paintings papering the houseboat's old walls were, to my eye, beautiful, realistic, and filled with emotion. I was a little overwhelmed by what seemed like unappreciated talent. At least unappreciated by a broader audience. Bud and Dorothy behaved like proud parents.

"Look at this, dear." Dorothy pointed to a charcoal sketch low on a bedroom wall. The drawing depicted a houseboat with a carved salmon on the front door—I was pretty sure it was Shirley's. A woman dressed in a business suit and heels stood on the deck facing the door. Her hair was drawn back in a swooping twist, and she carried a large, expensive-looking handbag.

"Is that Shirley's houseboat?" I asked.

Dorothy nodded.

"And who is the woman? Elaine Dupont?"

Dorothy turned to Geraldine. "Do you remember the woman in your painting? Was she that woman who wants to buy your home?"

Geraldine scrunched her face in concentration then shook her head and shrugged.

"Never mind," Bud said. "It doesn't matter. It's a fine picture; whoever the lady is." He patted her shoulder.

We moved to the next row where Geraldine pointed out several small pencil drawings of an older woman in a small sailing dinghy. A cat perched on the forward seat.

"Shirley and her cat?"

Geraldine nodded, her eyes blinked back tears.

I knelt down to examine the most recent additions. There was a pen-and-ink sketch of a man who looked a lot like Lawrence Winslow. He was walking away from Shirley's houseboat, head tilted down with just enough of his face showing to depict a scowl. I wanted to ask Geraldine about the drawing, however, the two elderly women were shuffling toward the door.

"They're getting tired," Bud said. "It's getting late. Time to go home, make dinner, get some rest." He reached down and offered his hand. "Come on, we can walk with Dot and get her settled and then you and I can walk to my place. I'm second to the end."

He was right—it was getting late and time for me to head back to *Ink Spot*. I figured I'd feed the cat, have a drink, and crash early. I wanted to try to have a personal chat with Lawrence Winslow in the morning, and I wanted to be fresh and rested for the attempt.

I reached for Bud's hand and was about to stand when I noticed one small pencil drawing in the very bottom left-hand corner of the wall. It couldn't have been more than four-by-four inches. The lines and shading were pale—almost translucent—ghost lines. I gasped.

The drawing was close to photographic in nature. There was no mistaking that the two people pictured were David Chen and yours truly. We stood in an intimate embrace, gazing steadily into each other's eyes. Bud chuckled when he noticed me staring at the drawing.

"Sometimes she makes things up," he said.

# 12

A buck-fifty won't buy a pack of gum from a vending machine, and it certainly won't buy much time from a Seattle parking meter. I figured I had about fourteen minutes to locate Winslow's office, bluff my way past whatever gatekeepers stood watch, endear myself to Shirley's old beau, gather information, and beat feet back to the street before yet another ticket covered the crack on Roger's windshield. Good thing I wore sensible shoes.

The fur-covered handcuffs I kept in my day pack slowed things down during a mandatory security check in the city building, but I managed to flirt my way past two bemused government guards and find the elevator with a full ten minutes to spare. I expected that a man in Lawrence Winslow's position would have the best view in the building. What I didn't expect, when I bolted off the elevator on the twenty-eighth floor, was to ram—with full body contact—into David Chen.

"Hey," he grabbed both my arms and held me in place. "Why the hurry?" Even with the height difference, our eyes met and lingered for a beat. "I'm guessing you're here to talk with Commissioner Winslow, right?"

He frowned. "This is police business. You should leave things to me."

"Let go." I squirmed and pulled back.

He released his hold while maintaining eye contact. He blocked my way. "I mean it, Ms. Blue. You don't belong here."

I narrowed my eyes and straightened. "Detective, port commissioners are elected by the people of Seattle. I'm a voter, and I have every right to visit an elected official whenever I wish."

In all honesty, I hadn't voted in years, and I suspected that ordinary citizens—even those who did vote—couldn't simply stroll in for a chat with an elected official whenever they wanted. But the meter was ticking. "Besides, I have reason to believe that Commissioner Winslow may have information that could help with my insurance investigation."

"I thought we agreed you would share your findings with me." Chen's frown deepened.

"Well, I haven't found anything yet. Nothing substantial. And, if I don't get moving, I probably won't have anything to report—now or in the future." I motioned for him to move.

Chen stepped aside and let me pass. "I expect to hear from you," he said. Then he dropped his voice so low I strained to hear. "In the very near future. Do you understand?"

I glared at him, didn't answer—just slid past him and hurried down the hall. I could feel Chen's eyes on me until I slipped behind the heavy oak door of Lawrence Winslow's outer office.

Normally, I'd have worked up some ever-so-blue-collar joke that would swoosh me past the posted rent-a-cop, and a new baby story that would glide me around a secretary's shield. At the moment, I had nothing. The time with Chen had not only slowed me down, it had also muddled my thinking, and that angered me. *He's a short, uptight cop, Blue. Get over it, already.*

Fortunately, I didn't need jokes or lines to breach Winslow's inner sanctum. He came to me.

"Hello." He held out his hand. Tall, sophisticated, real-looking tan, and a smile that probably put some orthodontist's kid through college. His grip was strong, steady, practiced. "You must be Kelly from the *Herald*. I've been expecting you. Come on in." Without waiting for a response, he glanced at his secretary.

"Hold my calls and visitors, Leslie." Then, I swear, he winked. The young woman blushed, nodded, and tapped a button on her desk phone. I made a mental note—okay, that's the game. Lawrence breezed by her, and I followed.

His office was more high-end CEO than what you'd expect of a local port commissioner. Three walls were solid glass with views of the entire county. There was a mahogany desk bigger than my bunk, a real leather sofa, a collection of overstuffed chairs, a wet bar, a coffee bar, and a treadmill. The one solid wall, paneled in dark wood, played host to a gallery of black-and-white photos—races, regattas, ribbon cuttings. Several shots—those mostly in color—highlighted Lawrence Winslow with celebrities and dignitaries. The place was meant to impress, and it did.

"Commissioner Winslow, these black-and-whites are extremely sophisticated. More art than—you know—more art than straight photography."

Lawrence beamed. "Nice eye," he said. "I do my own developing." He took a moment to gaze at his work and then pointed out several favorites. "Took that one from a helicopter over a race. Tough shot. I like the way it came out." He stepped close to me. "And, call me Larry. All my friends do."

"Nice angle," I said. Then pushing down a gag reflex, I fluttered my lashes, smiled, and added, "Larry."

Encouraged, he continued to mansplain his photographic techniques. "And this one, I deepened the tones—brought out the mood, don't you think?"

"Definitely. Brings out the mood."

We kept this up for a few more minutes until he seemed to remember that we were essentially strangers in a business meeting—not a couple attending an art opening.

"Well, enough about my silly little hobby," he said. "Can I offer you anything? Espresso? Tea? Glass of wine?" He motioned for me to take a seat next to a marble-topped coffee table. I smiled, shook my head, slipped out of my jacket and sat down. I'd learned it's harder to get the boot when you're seated.

He settled across from me poised to provide the right answers to whatever questions Kelly from the *Herald* asked. Except, she was, no doubt, waiting in the outer office.

"I'm sorry for the slight confusion," I said. "We haven't met yet. I'm Sheaffer Blue, an investigator with City Wide Insurance." I leaned forward, looked sincere and concerned. Larry couldn't help himself. There's something about a thin, low-cut T-shirt on a woman forty years younger that can distract even the most professional man. He glanced, then straightened, and cleared his throat.

"Obviously, my mistake. I've been waiting for a reporter. I'm not sure I understand why you're here, but you are, so what can I do for you?"

"Commissioner...uh, Larry," I smiled. "I won't take up much of your time, and I know you've got a lot on your plate right now with the bridge and all. It's just that I'm investigating the recent houseboat fire on Lake Union and, as I'm sure you know, a woman died in that fire. Our company, City Wide, is the insurer. We're trying to learn more about the circumstances. We are wondering if the bones in the bridge and the fire on the dock are somehow connected. We're trying to tie up loose ends. You know, for insurance purposes." I was totally winging it and hoping he didn't notice.

"Ah, the bridge." He made a dismissive gesture. "An old mystery. But the fire? A tragedy." His expression was one of rehearsed, civic concern. He waited for a moment. "I'm saddened for the community of course, though I'm not sure how I can be of help to you."

I could feel time and the situation slipping away, so I decided to dive in. "Well, I'm—that is, City Wide Insurance is—trying to determine if the death was an accident, or foul play, or something else. It will make a difference, you see, with the payout. And, we understand that you visited the deceased the day of the fire."

Larry stiffened. "I did. And I've told my story to the police already. She was an old friend. I was in the area on Port business and decided—pure whim—to stop by and say hello. I can't imagine what that has to do with the fire." He was careful and a little too defensive.

"That's exactly what we heard." I tried to use a reassuring tone. "'Old friend,' yes, of course. We're hoping you might have some insight—you know—in terms of her disposition that day. Did she seem depressed?"

"Ah, I see," he said. He leaned forward as if to share a confidence. "I wish I could help you. However, we—my old friend, Shirley, and I—didn't speak that day. I knocked and waited. No answer. The door was open, though, and well...we were buddies back in school, so I poked my head in." He paused, as if thinking things through. "Anyway—no Shirley. Her home was a mess. Stuff everywhere. I sort of thought, well...it almost looked like someone had ransacked the place. Then I remembered, she was a bit of a hoarder. She saved everything. Naturally, the place would be in shambles." He waited for a beat, then added. "Of course, it's been years...."

I matched his low, coconspirator tone. "We have reason to believe that maybe she was depressed. Maybe her death wasn't completely accidental. Maybe even...you know."

"That's exactly what I told the police," he said. "Low chance of foul play. Very likely an accident, or, maybe...what you said."

I started to seriously dislike the man, yet I tried hard to maintain a "we are in agreement" demeanor.

"You know," he said, "she was an elderly woman, and from what I understand her friends and neighbors have moved away from the dock. One, I think, moved to a retirement home." He shrugged. "And my guess is there might have been money problems. The place looked like it could use some work. Financial issues can be particularly hard on seniors. She might very well have been depressed enough to give up." He sighed. "We certainly do need to do something to help the elderly in this country." He cleared his throat and glanced at his watch.

I knew when a welcome was over. "I'm grateful for your insight," I said. "We'll probably have this wrapped up in no time. I think things are pretty clear." I shot him a smile, stood, turned to the view, and changed the subject. "This is really something. I love looking at the water and the boats from up here."

Larry rose and stepped next to me—too close for my comfort. "Are you a boater?" he said.

I gave an unintentional short laugh. "Sailor. Well, sometimes. I'm sort of 'in irons' at the moment. Financial issues can be hard on all of us." I held out my hand. "Thanks for your time and your thoughts."

We shook, and I started toward the door when I noticed the photo on his desk. A forty-something blond with perfect teeth, perfect hair, perfect everything. Could easily have been a supermodel in her youth.

"Your daughter?"

He laughed. "She'll get a kick out of that. No. That beauty is my wife. Beverly."

Lawrence Winslow waited until he was sure the young woman was in the elevator, maybe even out of the building. Then he made two calls. The first, on the interoffice phone.

"Leslie, I have a job for you. Find out everything you can about the woman who just left. Her name is Sheaffer Blue. She doesn't work for the *Herald*. Works for some local insurance company. I want to know her income, her financial standing, her education, background, who she dates, what she drives, what she wants out of life. Anything. Everything. And get back to me ASAP. Got that?"

Next, he punched a number on his private cell phone. He paced, chewed on his lower lip, gazed out his gleaming plate-glass windows while he waited for her to pick up.

"Hello?"

"Listen to me," he said. "I can't talk now but there is something you need to know. I'll call you tonight." Even though the room was soundproof as a tomb, he whispered his next words. "We have a problem."

# 13

I may not have formal training in insurance investigations or detective-type work, but I know enough about people, especially about men, to know when someone is lying. And I knew that Lawrence Winslow was in the middle of a big old fat lie. At the very least, he was hiding information. He knew a whole lot more than he'd shared. More about Shirley, the houseboat fire, and, I suspected, even more about the bones in the bridge. That's all I knew. And I didn't know what to do with what I knew.

My head hurt, and my stomach rumbled. Most of the time, when I felt like this, I'd wolf down whatever leftovers lacked mold, untie the lines, and head out for a sail. A couple of hours on the water could calm and soothe the most jangled of nerves. Even if *Ink Spot* and I only sailed circles around the lake, I would return renewed and ready to face the world. But *Ink Spot* was chained to the dock, and I was roped to reality.

I'd gone way past my allotted fourteen minutes of metered time, so I was outraged, however, not surprised to see Roger hoisted, hood-up, to a bright green tow truck.

94 · JESSICA H. STONE

Blue letters in Seahawk script spelled out Lou's Towing and Trash Removal.

Although I'd never seen him before, I guessed the short guy wearing green overalls was Lou. The ticket-issuing cop and I were drinking buddies, and luckily, I remembered his name. I sprinted toward the men.

"Jerry! I can't believe you're having me towed. Come on, let me off. I'll pay the fines."

He shook his head and closed his ticket book. "It's not just the pile of tickets you've ignored or the expired meter. This time you're parked in a handicapped spot. I can't help you with this, Blue. Sorry."

He did look sorry, and even though I was frustrated and pissed, I felt bad for him. It can't be easy having me for a friend.

The tow truck driver slapped a sheet of paper into my hand. "Pick it up any time after eight tomorrow. Have to show your receipt from the city and pay us. It's all on there." He clomped back to his truck. I watched as the tow truck pulled away with my Roger rolling along behind on his balding rear tires.

"Shit," I said. I turned to Jerry. "It keeps getting worse. I don't even have bus money right now."

He smiled. "I can help you with that. Come on."

On the drive to the marina, we shot the breeze, did a little flirting, and caught each other up on police department gossip. I asked Jerry to share any juice he might have on the investigation of the houseboat fire.

"Honestly, I don't know much," he said. "I feel like I'm nothing more than a glorified meter maid these days. They don't tell me anything. But there's one thing

I do know. You know that guy from California? The up-tight, fancy-dressing detective?"

I nodded.

"Well, the word is, he's got a thing for you." A big grin split Jerry's face.

I turned to look at him. "Like a good thing for me, or a bad thing?" I said.

Jerry's grin stretched wider. "Depends on your definitions of good and bad."

We joked around for a few more minutes until he pulled the squad car into the marina lot. With a promise to meet up for beers as soon as I could get my act together, I thanked Jerry for the ride and headed across the parking lot to my gate.

I must have been daydreaming because I almost stepped on Willie. He sat on the dock next to *Ink Spot* fussing with the padlock that held my boat captive. "Willie! Are you letting me off the hook?"

"Must have friends in high places," he mumbled. With a tug, he managed to release the lock. Together we slipped the chain from the boat.

"What happened?" I said.

"Some gal called with a credit card. A company card. Said to pay off your debt and pay for next month in advance. I didn't ask. Figured you'd know." With that, he looped the chain over his shoulder and shuffled away.

Free! I spent a few moments wondering who bailed me out. Chen? Why? Not too likely, even on a detective's salary. Besides, why would he? That made no sense. What about Spiderman? He was a big dufus, but hey, maybe surf shops turn a profit. After a couple more tries I decided it didn't matter. *Ink Spot* was free! I hopped onboard. The cat lay curled in a patch of late afternoon sunlight that spilled through a porthole onto the settee. He lifted his head and stared at me.

"Cat!" I said. "We're going for a sail!"

The cat looked up, blinked, yawned, and then, as only felines can, he stretched his entire body. I grabbed a handrail and swung into the saloon, sloughed off my jacket, and pulled my toolbox from under the companionway steps. My life might have been messy and my living space a minor disaster zone, however, my engine room was surgically clean. Always. Not a drop of transmission fluid dripped from my old Perkins diesel. Not even a thin sheen of oil floated on the shallow pool of fresh water under the pan.

Early on, I'd had the good fortune to learn diesel repair and maintenance from a crusty old mechanic. Earl could barely articulate his wishes at a fast-food drive-through window, but he could tease life into a machine that had lain rusting in the weather for decades. Old Earl considered every engine to be a sacred entity, and every engine room a temple. It was the first rule of boating that he'd shared with me, and it stuck.

The second rule was that a real boater never leaves the dock, never turns the crank, and never raises a sail without first testing all the fluid levels and opening all the appropriate valves. Doesn't matter how short the trip or how recently these things were done. Check everything. Every time. It was a rule I *never* violated.

After performing my duties, I fired up the Perkins. I wasn't surprised that it started immediately, although I was shocked that the cat didn't freak out at the rumble of the big engine. I'd expected him to make a mad dash for cover, flee in terror. Instead, he stayed put and calmly began grooming his private parts. Cats. Go figure.

We eased out of the slip and within minutes *Ink Spot* was mid-lake. I turned her bow to the wind and went forward to raise the main. Late afternoon was a perfect time for a sail—still enough wind to push the boat, enough sunlight to cast diamonds on the surface of the water, and, in the summer, close enough to evening for the moon to begin its journey. The sky was a watercolor of swirling pastels and a prism of shifting light.

When I hopped back into the cockpit, I found the cat snugged on a cushion on the starboard seat. From his comfortable position, he sniffed the air as if checking the weather and then calmly watched as I unfurled the jib. There was something sort of eerie and yet at the same time, sort of calming, about the way that cat reacted to the thunder of the engine and the groan of the lines as they stretched from clew to cleat. Shirley, I knew, had been in her stationary houseboat for decades and yet, the cat appeared perfectly at ease with the sounds and motions of an engine pushing sixteen tons of teak and fiberglass through the water.

I chatted with the big Tom as I coiled a line. "What do you know about Shirley? And how long have you and she shared a home? Were you a sailor's cat before you moved into that houseboat?" They were the kinds of questions I'd had since I'd first brought the critter onto *Ink Spot*. They were the kinds of questions, I suspected, I might never be able to answer. The cat yawned as if to say he was bored with this line of questioning. I shrugged and turned my attention back to the boat.

All sailors know about *the moment*, the quickening, the breath- and heart-stopping moment when the wind snaps the sails full and catches the boat in its embrace. In that second, the sailor is entirely, fully alive. In the next instant, when the engine stills, absolute peace takes hold, and the only sounds are the whoosh of water on the hull, the exhale of human breath, and the beat of the mariner's heart. I longed for that silence, for that magical moment, for that peace. When I turned the key and the engine hushed, instead of the anticipated quiet and calm, a long, high howl pierced the wind. It came from the cat. He stood on the companionway hatch balancing on all four paws, swaying with the boat's roll. With his head thrown back, he yowled up at the mainsail like a wolf at bay. No fear. No trauma. Full-on confidence. I glanced skyward—there it was—the ghostly light of the first of two full orbs to grace this month. I laughed out loud and joined him. There we were, girl and cat, howling at a pale blue moon.

We spent the next two hours circumnavigating Lake Union. We slid past restaurants and gazed at our reflections in their shimmery plate-glass windows. We squinted at the setting sun as it cut through glasses of chardonnay on outdoor tables, and we inhaled the greasy odor of grilled burgers and fries. It made me feel good to see that cat relaxed and content after the trauma he'd so recently survived. When I wasn't minding him, I focused on the wind, the rush of the water under our hull, the other boats, and the kayaks and seaplanes that shared the lake. Charred bodies, entombed bones, impounded vehicles, and financial woes were banned from my thoughts.

A jet passed overhead, and I watched it pen its trailing white signature against the Wedgewood-blue sky. It reminded me of the times I'd folded myself into an airplane seat—stiff like cardboard origami. I remembered when I'd silently and secretly joined a load of strangers as we collectively "helped" the captain brake when landing. I didn't fly often—only to visit close friends and only then when I could scrounge up enough cash for a ticket. I'd flown to hang out with my buddy Thom in southern California, and to Panama to roll around with an old lover, and once, to comfort my gal pal in Sydney, Australia, on the first anniversary of the death of her husband.

It didn't seem to matter how many miles I'd travel, or how many hours I'd been in the air, flying always left me drained, frayed at my edges and covered in a film of grime that begged an immediate shower. Sailing, on the other hand, calmed my worries, washed my woes. Whether I was out for a day, a weekend, or simply a few hours, I returned to land feeling as if I'd traveled to another country, experienced something new, seen the world through wondering eyes. The wind blew the grunge of exhaustion and stain of struggle right off me. The wind blew the stink away.

As I watched the plane disappear into piles of cumulus clouds, I renewed my personal vow to clean up my act, pay off my debts, and sail away. I glanced over at Shirley's cat now snoozing on a coil of line on the cockpit's sole. It occurred to me that I might have acquired my first crew member.

The air chilled, the wind calmed, and the sun nestled behind the mansions of Queen Anne. Late evening, and time to head back to the marina. I went forward to lower the main.

By the time I'd strapped the sail cover in place and rolled the jib snug, the lights of Seattle twinkled in the darkness. The cat pressed tight against the cushions. He shivered slightly in the cool breeze, but he continued to stay in the cockpit with me. I motored *Ink Spot* slowly, without a wake, back to our slip in Ballard Mill.

Sooty gray shadows of two men loomed at the head of my slip. I knew one would be a neighbor standing by to grab my lines. He turned and waved. I waved back. Then he shook hands with the other man and walked down the dock toward his own boat. I've pulled into my slip a thousand times, and for sure, on this windless evening I didn't need any assistance—still, I wondered why my neighbor left before he knew *Ink Spot* and I were safe and secure.

The other man, still only a dark silhouette, stood motionless for a moment and then he moved in closer to catch my lines. I didn't recognize him until he walked—until he limped. David Chen. My breath caught, and my heart did a quick two-step. Mortified by my reaction, I started to chide myself as *Ink Spot* began her slide into place, but in the next beat, I didn't have time to think about anything other than boat handling.

I nosed her into the narrow slip and tossed a line to Chen. He flailed around with his arms wide as if he were trying to catch a beach ball instead of a thin snake of rope. The line landed in the water, and he jumped back from the splash. *Geez. Landlubbers.*

Chen retrieved the line and gave it a hard tug, which pulled *Ink Spot's* bow snug against the dock, forcing her stern to swing dangerously close to the neighboring boat. Dangerously close to the costly crunch of fiberglass on fiberglass.

"Hey!" I yelled at him. "Ease off! Give it slack." I sprinted to the stern in time to push against my neighbor's railing and fend us off. Chen might have been a landlubber, but he wasn't a dummy. He obviously realized what was happening and eased his grip on the bowline. Then he hurried to the stern, and this time, he caught the line. I hopped off and secured *Ink Spot* snugly in her berth before turning to Chen. If the dock light hadn't burned out months ago, I might have been able to see the embarrassment on his face. Embarrassment his voice couldn't hide.

"Look, I'm sorry. This is the closest to a sailboat I've ever been. I just didn't think things through."

I wanted to read him the riot act, to go on and on about the damage he could have caused, to fuss and fume but honestly, I was feeling mellow from the time on the water, and his apology sounded genuine. "Oh, forget it," I said. "It happens."

We stood there for a moment, two shadows on a wooden dock on a cool dark evening. Finally, Chen cleared his throat. "I tried to call. Only got voice mail so I stopped by with the hope that we could compare notes about the fire. I have some information to share. And I think you may know something that I don't. Maybe we can help each other with this." He paused a moment and then stepped toward a package—a large vinyl bag on top of my dock box. He opened the bag and nodded toward its contents. "I brought cold beer," he said.

Most guys who want to ply me with beer just grab a six-pack from the local deli and swagger on down the dock. Not Chen. Chen had placed four bottles of an expensive microbrew on ice in the zippered cold bag. He'd even remembered to pack a bottle opener.

I hesitated. Thought for a moment. I usually turn my phone off when I'm on the water. Peace. Calm. No people. Other than what Mother Nature doles out, there's no chatter, stress, or drama. I didn't want to give up the peace I'd gained on the lake. Still, I was curious about what Chen had to say, and curiosity is a powerful motivator. Curiosity and cold beer. I gave in. "Sure. Okay. Come on board."

# 14

Chen stood next to the companionway steps clutching the bag to his chest as I zoomed around the salon grabbing up clothes, papers, and boat parts. Since my top-loading refrigerator no longer kept things cold, I figured it could at least serve as a quick and convenient storage unit. I propped it open with a broom handle. The smell of mold and something funkier wafted out. Ignoring the smells, I crammed a load down into the hole. Then I spun around, swiped my arm across the table, and swept my adult toy collection into a plastic bag. I tossed the bag in with the rest of the stuff, pulled the broom handle away, and let the top slam shut.

I turned to Chen. He'd plastered himself against the steps, looking as if he were more appalled with my squalor than he'd been with the death and destruction in Shirley's houseboat. He caught me staring at him and quickly turned away. I never really care one way or another what people think of my space, yet for reasons I couldn't fathom, I could feel my face warming and I imagined my cheeks flushing deep red. Now, it was my turn to avoid eye contact. I gestured toward the settee and cleared my throat.

"Well then," I said, "why don't you take a seat? Get comfortable." I turned back to the galley and rummaged in the cupboard for glasses. Can you believe it? Not one single clean glass or cup. Nothing. "Look..." I faced him. "I've been really busy lately. No time to clean up, or..." I shrugged and glanced toward the basin piled high with dishes.

"Never mind," Chen said. He squeezed into the narrow space on the settee behind the salon table and opened the bag. "We can drink from the bottles." He fiddled with the opener a moment and then noticed Shirley's cat. It sat on the floor in front of his feet and gazed up at him. "Is that the animal from the houseboat? I wondered what happened to him. Her?" He glanced down to where the cat was firmly seated. "I wasn't sure if it made it through the fire." He opened a bottle and handed it to me.

"Thanks." I took the beer. "He was in pretty bad shape, but he seems to be doing okay. Eats whatever I give him and he enjoys sailing."

Chen set his beer on the table, bent over, and gently lifted the cat onto his lap. He lowered his face and the cat lifted his until their noses touched. A rumbling filled the saloon. I sat and watched—gobsmacked.

"I take it you like cats." I tried to feign indifference.

Over the next half hour, I learned that both of Chen's parents had been veterinarians and that he'd grown up in a home filled with animals. "Our house was thick with cat and dog hair. I didn't like it. I didn't like the mess," he said. "That's why I don't have a pet of my own—the mess. And, of course, my lifestyle. Not much time to care for an animal. Even so," he said, then paused and peered closely at the cat's skin. "I miss them. Especially the cats." He looked up at me. "This guy is going to be just fine. His fur is already starting to grow back in. You're taking good care of him. Whatever you're doing, keep it up."

I bit my lip to keep from saying anything. I hadn't done much to help—I opened a can of tuna fish, took the critter for a sail. Still, I warmed from the praise. For the second time in less than an hour, I could feel my cheeks burning, and I felt, as I had before around this man, slightly confused. To clear my head, I tried to change the subject. "So, what about the fire? And Shirley? Accident? Can I turn in a report and get paid?" Chen shook his head and leaned forward for his beer. The cat jumped from his lap, leaving bits of flakey skin on his pressed, dark slacks. Chen made a face and brushed the flakes to the floor. Then he took a sip of beer, set the bottle on the table, and leaned toward me. In the soft, dim light of *Ink Spot's* salon, his eyes looked like deep pools of dark chocolate. I bit my lower lip. He studied my face. I hoped that the low lighting covered what I knew was a flush. I tried to make a sort of disinterested shrug—took a sip of my beer.

"It wasn't an accident," he said. "Maybe she was poisoned. The evidence isn't clear yet. However, we do know that the fire was deliberately set."

My stomach lurched. I gasped and snorted at the same time. Beer squirted from my nose, narrowly missing the front of Chen's shirt. He jerked back and then tugged a handkerchief from his pocket and offered it to me. I wanted to jump up and grab a paper towel or a wad of toilet paper, but I was wedged into the settee, so I snatched the square of clean white fabric from him. While I wiped beer and a bit of snot from my nose, Chen politely turned his attention to the cat.

"Are you a good boy?" He talked to the animal in that nauseatingly sweet baby-talk voice that people so often use with animals. Not something I would have expected from this seasoned detective. Then again, I really didn't know what to expect from this detective.

When I finished wiping up, I slipped the handkerchief into the pocket of my jeans. "I'll wash it and get it back to you," I said. Chen didn't seem to hear—he was leaning forward to scratch under the cat's neck. For a second, I felt a little surge of jealousy. Pissed at myself, I turned the feeling into irritation. I faked a cough, then spoke.

"So, tell me more about this murder theory."

Chen sighed as he straightened. He glanced at the cat one more time and then turned his attention to me. "As I said, I haven't pieced it all together. Yet." He kept on and on about evidence and things that didn't feel right and about the different theories he was testing. I was having a hard time concentrating. It occurred to me that I was within touching distance of a cop who I found confusing and irritating, a cop who'd brought me expensive microbrews, a cop I'd almost sprayed with nose goo, a cop who was describing the murder of an elderly woman, and a cop who wore an aftershave that, although I hadn't noticed it before, now made me feel slightly dizzy—not dizzy in a bad way—dizzy in that way that makes you want more. *More of what?* Chen stopped talking and leaned forward again, his face now only inches from mine. Then he smiled—not a big, happy sort of smile—more of a slow, "I got you now," sort of smile. I pretty much lost it and shut my eyes.

I had expected Chen to close the distance between us. I had expected him to press soft, warm, ever-so-slightly moist lips on mine. I had expected....

But what I got was the sound of a heavy thud, the crack of a bottle hitting the table and the shock of cold liquid splashing my shirt. Chen and I jumped at the same time. My bottle rolled and spilled into my lap. That damn cat sprang off the table as fast as he'd vaulted up onto it. The motion rocked the table, and Chen's bottle toppled over the side. Beer gurgled onto his polished loafers. Not what I'd expected.

While I fished around in the V-berth for dry clothes, Chen wiped his shoes. He'd grimaced when I'd offered him a dishtowel. He'd grabbed it out of my hands and went to work with a scowl. Clearly, this was not what he had expected either. I figured he'd lighten up. After all, it was only spilled beer—good beer, for sure—but not a bottle of say, hundred-year-old Scotch or a full fifth of Jack.

The only clothes I could find that weren't overly ripe were a pair of cut-offs and a purple Huskies sweatshirt. The cut-offs were splashed with dried bottom paint and sported several small acid burns from the times I'd topped up my batteries. The sweatshirt had one small pizza stain. Nothing too bad, I thought.

I felt pretty good, thought maybe we could walk to the deli and pick up more beer, maybe order a pizza. Maybe, after a couple more drinks, I could suggest that he probably shouldn't drive—just stay here on *Ink Spot*, crash on the settee or...I was actually starting to think there might be some possibilities with this guy.

I called to him from the closed V-berth. "So pretty funny when you think about it. Right?" I tugged the sweatshirt over my head. He mumbled an answer. I couldn't hear very well, so I flung the door open and jumped out. "Missed that—what'd ya say?"

Chen was halfway up the companionway ladder, his back to me. "I said, I didn't think any part of it was funny. And, I said I'll see myself out."

Damn. That stopped me cold. Why leave? Leave over a spilled beer? I started to argue but stopped myself. What was I doing? I rarely feel conflicted about men. For me, men are fun and titillating. When they no longer amuse me—or maybe when I wear them out—I simply move on. Men, I've decided, are like city buses. Miss one? There'd be another one coming along in ten minutes. Or accidentally board the wrong one and find yourself speeding in a direction you don't want to go? Just get off and wait. It won't be a long wait. On the other hand, Chen was leaving without so much as a kiss? I didn't get it.

I watched as he pulled himself to the top rung and stepped into the cockpit. Then I scampered up the ladder and stood next to the helm as he grasped the midship stanchion and tried to lower himself to the dock. His movements were awkward and jerky. *Okay.*

*Fine. Leave, you short little turd.* That's what I thought but what came out was, "Hey, just jump. Don't be a wuss. It's not that far." I knew my voice had a mocking tone and I didn't care.

The mast's shadow covered his face so I couldn't see his expression as he swung back and jumped. He landed and gave out a loud gasp. His right leg buckled and he hit the deck, knee first.

"Oh shit!" I hopped from the cockpit and down to the deck. "Hey, are you alright?" I reached out and tried to offer him support. He shrugged me off. With one hand pressed against the hull, he inhaled, gave a soft grunt, and pushed himself to stand.

"I'm okay," he said. His voice sounded strained. "I don't usually jump."

"You want some ice? Maybe you should come back on board. We can pull ice from your cold bag, and I have something stronger than beer to ease the pain." Again, I tried to touch him. This time he pulled away more forcefully.

"I'm fine. Really." It was clear he spoke through gritted teeth.

I dropped my arms to my sides. "Can you drive?"

Chen turned away and started up the dock. "Used Uber," he said, "I brought beer, remember?" He didn't turn, just kept walking. As he passed under one of the flickering dock lights, I noticed that his limp was more pronounced. His pain was obvious. I winced. I shouldn't have urged the jump. "Okay, I'll walk up the dock with you and wait for your ride."

"No!" He stopped and turned toward me. I couldn't read him—his face was a mask, his tone cool and dispassionate. "I'll touch base with you when I learn something new about the case, and hopefully, you'll honor our agreement and do the same for me. Have a good evening." With that, Chen turned and continued up the dock.

Well, another one bites the dust. Do not need another cop. *Especially not that one.*

When I figured Chen was ensconced in his ride and out of the area, I walked up the dock to the public bathrooms. Because the head in *Ink Spot* had been broken for over six months, nature's calls always required a trip up the dock.

The night was still and quiet, with no breeze to brush halyards into wind chime tunes, and no laughter from pockets of partygoers. Even the lone owl who nested in one of the brave little trees bordering the marina sat silent this evening. The only sound was the soft plat of my deck shoes on wooden slats.

The marina bathrooms at Ballard Mill are carbon copies of marina bathrooms around the globe—squat, concrete block structures house two toilet stalls, two coin-operated showers—one that drips continuously—and a small sink. Female boaters usually try to create a homey atmosphere by adding vases of plastic flowers and baskets of magazines, but despite their best attempts, the public heads in every marina I've ever visited are sad, smelly spaces.

I washed my hands, lingered a moment, and looked at myself in the mirror. My face should have been pink—flushed and healthy from the sail. But with skin colored by the fluorescent lighting in the stuffy, moist cave, the woman who stared back at me appeared ragged, frazzled, and stressed. In the short time I'd spent with Chen, my mood had changed a half-dozen times. Maybe it was the stress of seeing Shirley's body in that bag or learning that she'd been murdered. Or, perhaps the stress of having my boat, and then my car, impounded had something to do with this mood. Possibly, Chen's rejection stung more than I could admit, or maybe my shitty diet was catching up with me. Maybe I was simply worn out.

A basket of freebie magazines sported bright covers promising perfectly-posed models, celebrity gossip columns, and beauty tips. I considered snagging one before heading back to the boat. There were still two unopened beers in Chen's bag—I could drink one while I skimmed articles on the top ten ways to shed ten pounds before summer, or the top three things men want to hear in bed. I selected a glossy monthly, hesitated a second, and then dropped the magazine back into the basket. I knew I didn't want another beer and was pretty sure I wouldn't follow any tips on being the kind of woman every man wants. "Go home, Blue," I whispered to myself. "Go home and get some sleep. Tomorrow will be different."

Tired and ready to crash I sluffed down the dock. I had almost reached *Ink Spot* before I noticed the smell of cigarette smoke lingering in the still air. It struck me as strange because none of my neighbors smoked and I didn't see anyone around. Plus, I hadn't heard any footsteps other than my own. Of course, I'd been distracted, but it's hard to miss another person on a long wooden path four feet in width. A chill snaked up my spine; I shrugged it off. Never mind, I thought, someone has a guest for the night—a guest who smokes.

The cat had climbed into the cockpit and was perched on the companionway hatch watching shadows flit through the rigging. Bats. He made a little cackling sound deep in his throat. He seemed so happy that I decided to sit outside for a while and watch the bats with him. Maybe have one drink to slow my mind enough for sleep to come. "Hold that thought, buddy," I said. "Be back in a flash."

Below, I started for the cabinet where I stash my booze and my chocolate, and then I remembered the paddleboard instructor—Spiderman. Shit. We'd gone through my entire bottle of JD in one sitting and I'd finished off my emergency stash at Lilly's. If I'd had the cash I might have wandered up to the deli—it was open until midnight but moot point. No money. I stood in the salon and looked around. Chen must have been appalled at my living space. Even after my impromptu cleanup effort, the place was a total disaster. I stood there chewing on my lower lip trying to decide what to do when I noticed a shiny foil shamrock sticking up from the pages of my favorite book—*The Collected Poems of Langston Hughes*. My mother gave me the book on my twenty-first birthday. As far as I could remember, it was the only birthday present she'd ever given me. We weren't close. In fact, a deep appreciation of poetry and a full-on love of St. Patrick's Day were the only two things my mother and I had in common. Given my heritage—or at least what my mother thinks might be my heritage—the Irish holiday was a time for celebration, and I always threw a big bash to commemorate the wearing of the green. My friends, along with an odd assortment of strangers, looked forward to the fete and every year I ended up with a leftover stash of wine, whiskey, and several plastic containers of green potato salad from the deli. Last year someone left a full bottle of Tullamore Dew—an expensive and extremely smooth Irish whiskey. That one I'd hidden away in a secret place for just the right time. This seemed like the right time.

It took me a half hour to pull all the lines, sail bags, toolboxes, foul weather gear, and assorted bits of clothing from the V-berth and then another five to dig through the lazarette under the cushions. Eventually, I found the padded bag where I'd hidden the bottle. I crawled out and left cleaning up for another time. I grabbed a sweater, turned the lights off, and carried the whiskey to the cockpit.

With my back pressed against a cushion, I stretched my legs to rest on the wheel. The cat gave up his vigil and made his way to my side. He circled around twice like an old dog and then snuggled next to me.

"Hey, buddy." I gave his head a little pat.

The expensive stuff goes down smooth—no need for water or ice or anything else. Within minutes I'd mellowed enough to think about the past few days without feelings of stress. I thought about Geraldine and Dorothy and their pal, Bud. They hadn't shared anything I didn't know, except the bit about Shirley's relationship with Lawrence Winslow when they'd all been in college. And to be fair, that was a million years ago. But, it seemed strange to me that the port commissioner had paid a visit to his old friend on the morning before she died. Coincidence? David Chen probably didn't believe in coincidences. Maybe I didn't, either. The thought of the detective sent me down another rabbit hole until the cat yawned and brought me back. Something kept nagging at me. Something Chen and I had missed, but for now, it would have to wait.

In short order, the amber liquid worked its magic, and I almost nodded off before catching myself. I'd spent a lot of nights passed out in the cockpit, and it always meant waking up stiff and sore and covered with cold dew. Better to crash on my messy bunk. I stood, capped the bottle, scooped up the cat, and went below.

Before drifting off, I remembered that Shirley's friends had mentioned a fifth member of their old school gang, Charlie. He'd left Dock W and had moved to a retirement home because his wheelchair couldn't go down the steps and the dock association didn't have enough funds to pay to build a ramp. Although it was a long shot, maybe Charlie would have something to add to the story. Even a little bit might help.

I promised myself to call Lilly in the morning. She would drive me to the retirement home. Lilly loved old people and I knew she'd be wandering the halls, hugging seniors, and leading them in pagan chants or whatever wacko thing she was into at the moment. It would give me time to chat with Charlie and to pick his brain. Comforted by the idea of a productive task for the morning, and lulled by good Irish whiskey, I drifted off to sleep.

# 15

"So, what is our little problem, hmm?" Elaine Dupont tucked the phone between her shoulder and cheek while she pulled the cork from a bottle of merlot. She disliked her daughter's husband—considered him a weak, self-aggrandizing prick. A prick with a disturbing past. Still, he had money—lots of it. Her family had social pull, and money, plus influence, made for a profitable union. She'd all but arranged the marriage because, despite their differences and disagreements, she did love Beverly and wanted her to be happy. Happy and rich. So, putting up with, and keeping an eye on, Lawrence was her way of providing motherly protection for her daughter.

"That detective is fishing around. I know he suspects something. And I think he might be influencing the insurance investigator, too." Larry paused.

Elaine knew he was waiting for her to react and so she took her time as she poured a glass of wine, set the bottle down, reached for her phone, and tilted her head from side to side to stretch out the slight cramp from holding the phone. She took a sip and let the wine slide slowly down her throat.

"Are you listening to me, Elaine? This might be a serious problem. For both of us."

Elaine rolled her eyes. "It's not my problem. I haven't done anything, remember? You brought all this on yourself." She took another sip, closed her eyes, and relished the deep warm flavor. Then she went on. "Frankly, I don't see how this could impact me at all. The insurance investigator is getting pressure from her boss, that snot-snivel, Glen Broom. I saw to that. All she has to do is write a report suggesting a reasonable chance of suicide and case closed. I can move forward with the project. Simple."

"No, it's not simple, Elaine. I told you, that detective isn't buying the suicide idea. At least, not yet. And he's working on that insurance gal, too. Nothing we can do about him, but I might have a way to sway her—get her on our team, so to speak."

"I'm listening, Lawrence." Hearing his given name always made her son-in-law uncomfortable. Elaine imagined him cringing at the sound, and she smiled.

Larry cleared his throat. "I've done a little poking around. She's got a cash-flow problem and she wants to get out of town. Wants to sail her boat to Mexico. A little funding might go a long way to—"

Elaine interrupted him. "All right. You handle the immediate issues. I'll make her an offer—give her an incentive to help her speed up her report writing. Maybe I'll hold a little soiree at your house. Something to impress upon these little people the kind of power they're dealing with." She held her glass up to a light and swirled the ruby liquid. "Now, if that's all, I'm signing off, as I truly am busy this evening." She didn't wait for him to respond.

# 16

*It is the dawning of the Age of Aquarius...A quaaarie us....*
"Oh, God." I groaned, and without opening my eyes, I reached out from under my comforter and groped around the bunk for the phone.

*A quaaarii us....*
"Damn it. Where the hell is that phone?"

The music stopped, and I knew Lilly was leaving a message in her sweet, singsong voice. I didn't need to listen. I needed to find my phone, unglue my eyes, and hit redial. Finally...contact. As I waited for Lilly to pick up, I made a mental note-to-self—at night, expensive Irish whiskey coats the throat smooth as silk, by morning, it scratches like an old wool sweater. That thought led me to wonder, as I have on many mornings in the past, why some booze leaves me shaky, others leave me without memory, and others, like the stuff I found hidden away last night, give me that "run over by a truck" feeling. I had started a second mental note—to discuss this weighty question with one of my favorite drinking buddies—when Lilly picked up.

"Blue? Oh, Blue. You won't believe it. It's so awful...I don't know what I'm going to do...my uncle's pets, all my artwork...the garden, my students, and it isn't fair and they didn't even consider and...." She paused long enough to suck in a deep breath before spouting out, "can they even *dooooo* that?" She sucked in a sob.

"Lil, calm down, girl. Breathe. Isn't that what you're always telling me? Breathe." I held my cell phone scrunched between my jaw and shoulder as I rummaged through the galley cupboards trying to find something—anything—that resembled coffee. The best I could come up with was an open, half-can of cola. I squinted at it, not sure how long it had been hiding behind the dishes in the sink.

"I *am* trying to be calm but this will wreck everything and I have so many bills and if I can't teach classes in the studio I'll go in debt and they'll put me in prison and the rats will bite me and I'll get rabies and lockjaw and I'll never get to finish my poem about cosmic camouflage and...and...." Now she was full-on sobbing.

Although I had no idea what she was talking about, I could tell this was clearly an important issue—at least *she* felt it was important. And, because she's my closest friend, that meant whatever it was, it was important to me, too. "Lilly, try to breathe, honey. You know I'm here for you. We'll deal with this together." I swirled the liquid around in the can and listened. The fizz was gone. I hoped the caffeine remained. "Tell me, slowly. What is the problem? Who are they?"

Instead of spelling out the issue, Lilly went into another crying jag, her long sobs punctuated with honking and snorting as she blew her nose. I gave her a moment, gulped the soda. Even warm, and without the fizz, it had the same unmistakable cola flavor. It slid on down easy. Would have been better with rum. Even so, it did the trick. I took another swig and then tried a different tact with Lilly.

"Look, girl, I need your help today. I need you to drive me to a retirement home up on Queen Anne. I have to interview some old dude for my case, and Roger is in the pound. I sure could use your help. That is if, you know, you can manage."

Lilly perked up. I knew she would. She always wants to help me, no matter what the project, plus, she heard the words "retirement home." One time she told me that the elderly lack the self-consciousness of younger people because they have no problem laughing at themselves if they get tangled in a tango class or if their ceramic coffee mug collapses in the kiln and comes out looking like a smashed ashtray.

"Okay." She sniffled. I could hear the change in her voice already. "Give me about a half hour and meet me in the marina parking lot."

"That's my girl," I said. "See ya soon. You can tell me all about it on the way."

As I waited for Lilly, I made a hasty decision. I searched through my phone's contacts and found Chen's number. Even though I felt like a silly high school girl with a crush on the football team's star player, I left him a cheeky, and not at all sophisticated, text message. The second I hit "Send" I felt regret. Strangely, I also felt elated.

*You have got to cut down on the drinking, Blue,* I chastised myself. *Get more sleep. Exercise. Start eating better. 'Cause, girl...something is seriously messing with your brain.*

On the drive to the Evergreen Gardens Retirement Home, Lilly explained why she'd been so upset.

"I got a notice from the City of Seattle and a letter from the Magnolia Neighborhood Council," she said. "Apparently there is some ancient bylaw about no military structures allowed in residential neighborhoods. The City says my Quonset hut is a military structure and I have thirty days to remove it from the property or they are going to come and destroy it."

I could tell she was warming up to another tidal wave of tears, so I asked her about the letter.

"Well," she held back a sniffle, "according to the letter from the council, one of my neighbors circulated a petition about having Uncle Marv's pets removed from my roof. They said the pets posed a health hazard... something about someone getting hurt if one of the cement animals fell off the roof...and that they were not in keeping with the general appearance of the rest of the community. I think that's wrong. Those animals have been up there for decades, and actually, they bring a little fun and joy to that beige-on-beige suburb." She shook her head and pounded the steering wheel. "Anyway, when the city inspector came by to look at the pets, he noticed the Quonset hut and declared it a military structure. The letter said that everyone—without exception—signed the petition."

"Did *you* sign the petition?" I said.

She glanced over at me. "Of course not. This is the first time I've even heard of it."

"Well then," I said, "obviously there was *at least one* exception."

Lilly sighed. "So, what does that mean?"

"It means, girlfriend, that if there is one exception, there are others." I grinned, reached over and patted her arm. Although the bit about exceptions didn't mean anything, it was the only thing I could think of to calm her down. I had absolutely no idea how to help Lilly with this problem. To be honest, I was a little surprised that the city had let the eggplant stay in place for as long as it had. They probably did have the right to enforce building codes of some kind. I wasn't sure if there was anything I could do, especially because Lilly was right about one thing—no question about it, her neighborhood was a creamy shade of vanilla.

A handsome but slightly frazzled and clearly overworked nurse met us at the reception desk. He introduced himself as Ray and told us he was in charge of the night shift but that he would stay on a few more minutes and take us to Charlie. We signed the Visitor's Form and followed Ray down a long hall to the recreation room.

"Charlie is probably watching the financial news," he said. "That man is one of the sharpest of our residents. If he could move around without the chair, he wouldn't be in here. I wish there was something I could do to get him back to his old home. That houseboat of his is all the old guy ever talks about. Well, that and the stock market."

We found Charlie dressed in clean, pressed khaki slacks, a pale blue shirt, and a blue and tan vest. He wore a perfectly knotted navy bowtie. As Ray had expected, the dapper old man sat glued to the stock market report, although he immediately clicked the remote off when he learned he had visitors. Once the introductions were over, Ray excused himself. Lilly wandered off to visit with a group of ladies that she said, "seemed like they could use some yoga exercises." Charlie and I were left to chat.

"I'm so sorry about your friend," I said. "Such a tragic accident. It must have been a shock to all of you."

Charlie snorted. He snarled with contempt. "Accident my 401(K). Shirley was rubbed out. No question about it. That was no accident. Shirley was murdered."

I took a step back. I hadn't expected this from the tidy accountant in the wheelchair. "Are you sure? I mean...what makes you even think that?"

Charlie looked at me for a long time before he spoke. "Whose side are you on, Miss Blue?"

Now I took my time before answering. "Officially, I'm an insurance investigator," I said. "But something about this whole thing seems off. I've been taking care of Shirley's cat and judging by the calm, self-confident manner of that critter, I'd guess that Shirley was a kind and straightforward person. Probably never hurt anyone or anything. So, if it wasn't an accident...well, Shirley deserves...deserved better."

Charlie hesitated. He seemed to be weighing his thoughts. Finally, he motioned for me to follow him.

"Let's go to my place," he said. "It's quiet there, and we can talk in private. There is something you need to know."

Charlie's room was clean and orderly. A wooden rack held current issues of the *Financial Times, The Wall Street Journal,* and *The New York Times.* A small corner desk supported an older model laptop connected to a blinking modem, a dot matrix printer, and a National Public Radio promotional ceramic mug filled with pens and pencils. A legal pad covered with numbers and formulas written in pencil lay next to the computer. Charlie, I guessed, worked to keep his mind sharp.

I closed the door and sat down on a padded folding chair across from him. "So, what do I need to know?"

Charlie cleared his throat and began his story. "This goes a long way back, to when we were in college." He glanced up at a framed black-and-white photo on the wall.

I wanted to get up and study it, but I didn't want to stop his flow, so I stayed in place and nodded.

"You probably already know that Shirley and that fellow, Lawrence—we called him Larry—Winslow, were an item. Unlikely pair. Shirley was a couple of years older and had her act together. That kid was getting his feet wet, didn't even drive a car, rode a bicycle everywhere. Half the time Shirley rode on his handlebars. Of course, they looked ridiculous but none of that mattered to Shirley. Once they hooked up, you'd have to use a crowbar to wedge them apart. For some reason, she had a thing for the young pup so we all went along with it."

Even though I'd already heard this part of the story, I nodded and leaned in to show my interest.

"Well," he said, "I'm guessing that you already know that part."

The old man was sharper than I'd given him credit. I must have blushed.

"Thought so," he said. "But what you don't know is that Shirley and Larry, well, something went down the night of his twenty-first birthday. Something bad. And that thing caused the two of them to split and never reconnect. Their breakup—or maybe that thing, whatever it was—made Shirley give up on love for the rest of her life." He paused a moment before continuing. "Of course, it's not like we didn't try to help her back into her sexy, fun-loving self." He smiled softly, seemed to be remembering something. He shook his head as if to clear the thought. "Anyway, whatever went down that night changed Shirley's life. Changed all of us, a little." He glanced back up at the photo.

This time, I stood and walked over to it. Six friends—kids, really, college buddies smiling big, silly twenty-something smiles. Dressed in bell-bottomed jeans and tie-dyed shirts, they looped arms around each other and flashed peace signs with their free hands. Faded and cracked black-and-white memories. Behind me, Charlie sighed.

"Good times. Those were good times."

I returned to my chair. "What do you think happened?"

"I have my suspicions," he said. "But I made a vow to Shirley to keep my thoughts to myself. She said we had to protect the others and that we had an insurance policy that would take care of us until the last one dropped.

She said it was the best gift she could ever offer and that we had to protect it."

This time when I leaned forward, the interest was not only sincere, it was heightened. Broom had mentioned that he'd tried to sell Shirley an insurance policy, but that Shirley hadn't seemed interested. Lack of insurance and lack of beneficiaries was a big hang-up in processing this claim and moving on with Elaine Dupont's scheme. That, and oh yeah, David Chen's hunch about murder.

"Insurance policy?"

Charlie nodded. "But not the kind your company issues. I think Shirley had something more important than that. She had some sort of information that she could use to stop the entire dock renovation project." He shouted the words when he spoke of Elaine Dupont's construction plans. He gripped the arms of his wheelchair until his knuckles whitened. "And she wanted to share it with me. We had an appointment to meet. She was coming out here to discuss what to do. She said she needed to show me something. Said she needed my help. Maybe get a lawyer if it came to that. She said she knew she could trust me."

I watched Charlie's face relax with his last sentence. I let him stay with his thoughts for a few moments until I couldn't wait anymore.

"Well, what was it? What did she show you?"

Charlie exhaled. "That's the thing of it. She died before she got here. From what I've heard, her houseboat was trashed in that fire." He shrugged. "Chances are we'll never know."

I thought for a bit and then asked another question. "Could she have a safety deposit box? Maybe she put the policy, or whatever she had, in a bank for safekeeping. If so, maybe the key is still around. On a keychain. Or, maybe she gave one of the others a copy?"

Charlie shook his head. "No, not a chance. Shirley didn't trust the banks, and I don't think she would ever have shared her secret with anyone except me. I know she had something special—something important. I don't know what it was or where she stored it, but I'm positive it wouldn't be in a bank." He chuckled softly. "Knowing Shirley the way I did, I'll be willing to bet she hid it in plain sight—someplace where no one would ever think to look."

We sat alone in our thoughts for a few minutes. Finally, I cleared my throat and spoke. "Some people suspect that she might have been depressed. That she might have...you know."

"The hell with that!" Charlie slapped his palm against the arm of his wheelchair. "Shirley would no more off herself than she'd drill holes in the floor of her houseboat and sink it. That woman loved life. And she had the soul and spirit of a fighter. No way would she even consider something as cowardly as suicide." He trembled with rage.

Nervous that he'd pop a gasket or something, I tried to change the subject. "So, are you going to sell your houseboat? Couldn't you use that money for...your retirement?"

Charlie gritted his teeth and clenched his fists. His face turned a deep wine color, and then he pounded on the arms of his chair. It was clear that my attempt to calm him wasn't working.

"That harpy will never—*never*—get my home. She'll have to kill me to get my piece of the dock!" He leaned forward and spat his words. "I'll let those young boys stay there until they are grown and have kids of their own if that's what it takes." He was so worked up I was afraid he would tumble out of his wheelchair. I started to stand to catch him. "And, mind you, missy— Geraldine and Dorothy are steadfast in this, too." He started coughing and raised his voice. "And Bud, too. That evil woman will not, I tell you, not get our dock!" He coughed and shook so hard I freaked out. I reached over to the bed and pressed the call button and then started pounding on Charlie's back.

"Water? Do you want some water?"

Before I could do anything else and before Charlie choked to death, Ray came bursting into the room. Lilly trailed after him. Ray seemed to have superpowers when it came to soothing upset people because, within a few minutes, he'd settled the elderly man down and had arranged for Lilly and me to join Charlie for lunch in the dining hall. Lilly and I followed Ray as he pushed Charlie's wheelchair down the hallway.

I nodded toward the nurse's back. "Thought he was off work," I spoke softly in Lilly's ear.

"He stayed to show me around." She flushed a deep pink and nodded. "Cute, huh?"

I glanced at Ray as he bent to push the wheelchair up a ramp into the dining hall. "Well, nice butt," I said.

Lilly grinned and gave me a light smack on the arm.

Charlie used the lunch period to show off his two new visitors. We met about a dozen elderly folks, all gushing over Charlie's new "young people." It was clear I wasn't going to learn any more about Shirley's secret insurance policy, so I just went along with the hugs, the smiles, and second helpings of creamed soup, mashed potatoes, and tapioca pudding.

# 17

I'd hoped to get Lilly to drive me back to the marina so that I could take a long after-lunch nap, but a call from the clown changed that plan.

"Sheaffer, get over to the office ASAP." Broom sounded like he was in a bad mood, or seriously stressed out. "You need to give me a full, official report. I don't have anything to give our client yet, and she's breathing down my neck. She wants a progress report now!"

I sighed. "Okay, Glen. Calm down. I'm on my way."

"Sheaffer. I mean it. Now!" With that, the clown ended both the call and my plans for a quiet afternoon.

"Did you see how kind he was with those old people? And how he listened to everything they said? He was so careful to lift them gently and slowly—they bruise so easily, you know, and did you hear the way..." Lilly continued to babble on nonstop on the entire trip to the City Wide office. She made it crystal clear that Nurse Ray had made a significant impression. And it didn't take a super shrink to see that Lilly was over-the-top smitten with the guy. Silly woman.

I stopped listening after the first five minutes—that sort of girly-girl gushing gives me cramps, and besides, I was busy working out what I was going to tell the clown. He wanted a report—a report that would satisfy Elaine Dupont's "request" that Shirley had taken her own life. A nice, tidy little wrap-up that would give Elaine the green light to go ahead and bulldoze—at least figuratively if not literally—the remaining holdouts—Geraldine, Charlie, Dorothy, and Bud. In other words, he wanted a report that I knew I could not give him.

Glen Broom and I were the only ones who worked at City Wide, so I wasn't surprised to find the tiny receptionist's desk unoccupied when I arrived. I was, however, a bit concerned to find Broom's office empty, as he rarely leaves it unless to shuffle through papers on my desk. He wasn't there, either. In fact, the dingy, old, one-story building was wide open and unlocked. This seemed a bit strange as the clown is one of the most paranoid people on the planet. I shrugged it off, slipped out of my jacket, tossed it over the back of my desk chair, and flopped down. First things first: a quick check of my phone. No new calls. No new texts. Shit. *Shouldn't have sent that stupid text.*

I'd barely started reviewing the photos of Shirley's houseboat when Broom rushed in waving Seattle's daily newspaper. I glanced at the clock on the wall and frowned—tried to give the impression I'd been there a long time and had been waiting for my colleague to show for our meeting. Broom missed my act entirely.

"Sheaffer!" He slapped the paper down on my desk and gulped for breath. "Look at this! What do you think of this?" He crashed down into the straight chair opposite my desk and clutched his chest as he wheezed for breath.

I stared at him a moment, then leaned forward. "Glen, get a grip. You don't look so hot."

He shook his head and pointed to the newspaper. "Look. Look."

I glanced down at the paper expecting to see some massive car crash or collapsed building as Broom was always pointing out "important insurance incidents" to me. There, on the front page, was a full-color shot of what looked like a team of archeologists excavating a crumbling column with small tools and paint brushes. The headline read—*Bones Found in I-90 Bridge Identified as Former Port Commissioner.*

"News." Broom pointed first to his watch and then to the ancient television on top of the filing cabinet. "Turn on the news."

I turned on the television to an interview in progress.

"So, how is your wife taking this, Commissioner Winslow?" A young reporter leaned forward and thrust a mic in Lawrence Winslow's face. "The deceased was her grandfather, isn't that correct?"

Lawrence Winslow took a step backward while keeping his professional composure.

The reporter pushed on. "The deceased was also a port commissioner, isn't that right? And there was a big investigation at the time, but the body was never found. Do you have any thoughts about that?"

Winslow cleared his throat and looked directly, meaningfully, and oh-so-sincerely into the camera. "I am working with local law enforcement to provide anything the port can offer. I feel confident that our highly trained officers will be able to shed more light on this situation in the very near future. In the meantime, I would ask the media and the general public to respect the privacy of my wife and her family. As you can understand, this is an upsetting discovery. That's all I have at this time." With that, Winslow held up his hand and turned away.

The reporter faced the camera and signed off with, "Back to you, Jennifer."

The anchorwoman wrapped up. "We'll be following this and all important local stories and, as your leading news information program, we'll keep you up to date on any breaking developments."

An advertisement for ultra-soft toilet tissue rolled across the screen. I clicked the television off and turned toward Broom.

"And this is important to us, why?"

The clown ranted and paced and went on and on. He kept whining that if something impacted the port it might put a stop to Elaine Dupont's project and that might mean she'd pull out of City Wide and oh the pain and agony—the pain and agony. I slipped into my "I'm paying attention, and I'm so concerned" mask and went for a peaceful mental sail around the lake. Eventually, Glen wound down and made some pathetic squeaking noise that brought me out of a mellow trance.

"Well, we're on it, boss," I said. "We're doing everything we can. No one can fault us for that." I'd learned a long time ago that words to that effect—words that meant absolutely nothing at all—usually worked to defuse most situations. This time was no exception.

"I didn't think you'd understand, Sheaffer." Glen sighed. "But it makes me feel very good that you do get this. You really are becoming part of our City Wide team." He looked at me with watery eyes. "I had my doubts about you but..."

He carried on for a few more minutes, and I made more soothing sounds, and finally, he mopped the last of the sweat from his face and gestured toward the door. I almost made it out, reasonably unscathed, when Glen called me back.

"Oh, in all the excitement I almost forgot." He tossed a large, cream-colored envelope at me.

"What's this?"

"Invitation. Cocktail party at Port Commissioner Winslow's house. You have to go."

"What? I don't get it."

"All the employees at City Wide were invited, which means both of us. But it's my thirty-fourth wedding anniversary. Some ground is sacred. Besides, the wife would kill me if I didn't take her out. That means it's up to you."

"But why would they have a cocktail party right after digging Gramps out of his concrete boots?"

He shrugged. "Rich people are strange. Not my problem. You're on the team. You go."

I sputtered. "Glen, I don't have a dress or shoes or anything to wear to something like that. Hell, I don't even have transportation right now. I can't do it."

Broom fished his wallet from his back pocket and pulled out two twenties. He handed the bills to me. "Here. This will get you a taxi. And, I want a receipt."

I snatched the money and jammed it into my pocket.

"Now, you better get going because the party is tonight. In about three hours." Broom looked up at the clock as he turned and shuffled back toward his office. He paused and looked back at me once more. "You're on your own for the dress," he muttered.

# 18

David Chen leaned down, rubbed his leg, and silently chastised himself. The leap from the sailboat had been a stupid—no, an idiotic—act. What had he been thinking? He shook his head, straightened, and then twisted back and forth at his desk to loosen tight muscles. Finally, he closed the folder he'd been reading and pushed it to one side. He glanced at the clock—it was getting late. Trader Joe's would be closing in an hour, and he needed groceries. More than that, he needed a good bottle of wine.

He gathered up the files he'd been working on, slipped them into his desk drawer, and locked it. There wasn't anything particularly sensitive in any of the files, but locking up was a habit.

"I'm heading out, now." He gave a half wave to the two other detectives still working at their desks. "See you guys bright and early." The others nodded without looking up from their work. "Right." Chen mumbled under his breath. He knew that when they finished their reports, they'd wind up the day with beers at the brewery around the corner. And he knew that if he pressed, they'd invite him to go along. He also knew that wasn't going to happen. They would go out, do the guy thing, and then go home to their wives or girlfriends. He'd go back to the apartment, sip wine alone, read, and then go to bed. Alone.

Trader Joe's bubbled with voices, laughter, and clanging bells. Even an hour before closing, carts jammed the narrow aisles as shoppers selected from a wide variety of specialty cheeses, smoked fish, frozen appetizers, and the hundreds of tasty, unnecessary food items carried in the upmarket food chain. Chen pulled a folded sheet from his wallet. He never shopped without a list. His lists were ordered in a specific way—items organized into groups—different types of pasta listed together, capers, olives, and oils together, meats in another group, produce in another. On the extremely rare occasions when someone saw one of his lists, he endured a ration of teasing. Chen didn't care about the ribbing as he found the organization efficient and time-saving and, because he didn't have to spend much mental energy on selecting items, he could use the rather mindless activity of grocery shopping to mull over particularly vexing issues. Issues like the current case.

He excused himself and reached behind a man and woman who stood in front of a display debating the differences between virgin and extra virgin olive oil. He grabbed the brand he always used, placed it in his cart, and maneuvered down the aisle. Today had been both productive and disappointing. He knew he'd discovered clues. He knew he had information that could shed light on the houseboat fire/murder case and that was good. He didn't know exactly what those clues were or how that information played into the bigger picture, and that was troubling. He had a working theory, but he couldn't quite connect the dots. Not yet, anyway.

Pausing in front of the chips and crackers display, Chen mentally reviewed the day. He started with a conversation he'd had with his current partner, Gary Washburn. Gary and he had been temporarily paired in Seattle while their permanent partners had paired—temporarily—in San Francisco. The whole exchange program had been something concocted by the Public Relations Departments of the two police units. The idea was to swap lead detectives for a month—infuse new techniques, bring fresh energy into both organizations.

The four detectives and most of the beat cops in both cities thought the program was a waste of time and money but for whatever reasons, the brass loved it. So, Chen and Gary were a team—at least for the rest of the month.

He and Gary had learned from the folks in forensics that the skull found in the I-90 bridge had been struck by a triangular object. Further, from the arrangement of the bones, it looked as though the former port commissioner had been in a sitting position, probably on the edge of the wooden frame, and had either fallen, or was pushed, backward into the hole. The two men had theorized about the case over lunch in the station's staff room.

"My guess is that he was already dead and his assailant, or assailants, pushed him up and over the frame and then covered the body with the hope that it would be buried under cement when the bridge column was poured." Chen took a bite of cold smoked salmon.

"I'm betting on a crime of opportunity." Washburn attacked his triple-decker beef sandwich. "Probably drugged-out vagrants saw a well-dressed man, clearly out of his environment, wandering around the construction site and smashed his skull. Easy prey. Easy money."

"I'm not convinced." Chen shook his head.

"Well look, except for his wedding ring and that tie pin with the city seal on it, there was no jewelry, no wallet or credit cards, and no other items at the scene. Robbery makes the most sense."

"Maybe. You might be right. When I interviewed his daughter, Elaine Dupont, she said that her father had gone missing the night of a big party. She admitted being at the party and being underage and drinking. She said she's always wondered if her father had been looking for her when he went missing but that's all she knew. Her story checks out with the police report from the time. I think the commissioner was out looking for his daughter and ran into something he couldn't handle."

Gary nodded. "Exactly. Probably thought his kid was making out down by the water and went to get her—fatherly thing to do. But someone nailed him. Wrong place. Wrong time."

Chen had disagreed with his partner. It didn't feel like robbery although he didn't know why. "What about Shirley Cantrell and Lawrence Winslow? We know they went to the site around the same time. I think there's more to this," he said, arguing his point.

While his question was reasonable, Washburn had reminded him that, on a hunch, they'd interviewed everyone they could find who'd been at that party decades ago and that, like the others, Winslow had an alibi.

Winslow had admitted to being at the party and to leaving early to follow the former commissioner to the construction site. He admitted that he'd made a big scene, told everyone he was going to teach that politician a lesson about barging into private parties and private lives. He'd admitted, sheepishly, that he'd been trying to impress his girlfriend, Shirley Cantrell, with his macho display of activism. But, he'd been adamant about this— he and Shirley never made it to the construction site. With a good-old-boy sort of grin, he'd implied that he had borrowed his father's car for the occasion and that he and Shirley had made good use of the backseat of the big old Buick. The alibi wasn't airtight. Still, with no other witnesses, and Shirley now lying in the morgue, Winslow's word would have to stand.

Chen sighed and pulled himself out of his mental review. He reached for a box of water biscuits and then moved out of the way of a woman who pushed a cart full of noisy children down the narrow aisle. He moved to the wine section, gazed at the reds, and tried to decide on which vintage would go well with the cheese and olives he'd already selected. Generally, this was a pleasant task, but he kept losing his train of thought, kept drifting back to something that had happened late that afternoon. Wasn't anything significant so far, yet the memory of it lingered. He slipped back into his review of the day.

He'd gone back to the crime scene for another look around. He'd started in the bedroom—stood by the bed, tried to get a feeling or notice something he'd missed before. Nothing. He'd moved to the main room and, in the dusty rays of sunlight that filtered through smoke-smudged windows, he slowed his breathing, released tension, and had quietly observed. He'd been through this room before, twice now. The first time that disheveled insurance woman with the strange name and her cell phone's annoying ringtone had distracted him. Even now, thoughts about her continued to addle him. He grimaced at the thought of Ms. Sheaffer Blue—she was bad news. Best to avoid any more interaction. Best to send Gary if they needed to contact the red-headed insurance investigator. Then, despite his better judgment, he reached for his cell phone and clicked to her text. This was at least the fifth time he'd read it, and it still made him grin.

When he'd looked up from the phone, he'd noticed something different—something that had changed since the last time he'd been there. Three dark patches on the faded wallpaper indicated that things had been hanging there for a long time. He initially remembered seeing photos and some kind of stitchery. Now, except for the dark spots, the wall was bare. The debris on the floor yielded two of the three missing items. He made a note to review the photos the crime scene team had taken—they would show what had been hanging there the morning after the fire.

"Excuse me?" A tall, thin woman dressed in pink leotards, a lavender sweatshirt, and expensive trainers pointed to the shelf of wine behind him.

"Oh, sorry. Daydreaming." Chen cleared his throat and moved to one side.

The woman ignored his comment, grabbed a couple of bottles, and spun away in an obvious hurry. Chen shook his head and focused on the wine selection. He chose a label he knew and liked, paused, then reached for a second. He placed the bottles in his cart and checked his list—one package of hand-pressed ravioli and he'd be done. His leg throbbed and his head hurt. He was ready to go home and open the wine.

As always, vehicles had choked Trader Joe's parking lot when he'd arrived so Chen had parked his rental in an alley behind the store. Following habit and common sense, he paused and surveyed his surroundings before opening the trunk. Other than a faint hint of cigarette smoke—unusual in this upscale, politically correct neighborhood—the area seemed quiet and peaceful. For a moment he wondered if temporary housing in the burbs might be a better choice than his current place overlooking the city. Maybe it would get him away from work more—away from constantly thinking about crime. Maybe he could even spend a little time thinking about being a father—doing all the things fathers do. He shook his head and dismissed the thought—the assignment was temporary—he'd stay where he was. Chen grabbed two bags from the cart, turned, and bent slightly to lower them into the trunk. That's when the bullet hit the trunk lid and seared across his arm.

# 19

Instead of using Broom's cash on a cab, I called Lilly. It wasn't fair of me to keep asking her for rides, so I promised myself I'd make it up to her somehow or another. I didn't know my opportunity to give back would come so quickly.

On the ride to the marina, I shared Glen's story and the news about the identity of the bones in the bridge. Lilly drove and listened without interruption. When I got to the part about being forced to go to a cocktail party for rich people and about not having anything to wear, Lilly lit up. She turned the steering wheel so abruptly the tires squealed, and I slammed against the car door.

"Hey!" I grabbed at the dash and righted myself.

"This is great news! I've always wanted to doll you up and now is my chance!" My friend beamed and bounced in the driver's seat.

I gripped the dash, held on tight, and glanced over at Lilly as she raced toward Magnolia. For the first time that day, I noticed her outfit. She wore an ankle-length satin skirt with panels in four different tones of green, gold, and scarlet. A baggy, open-knit sweater in dark maroon hung loosely over a sparkling orange tank top. Ropes of beads and bells dangled from tangled strands, and long silver threads, woven into the shapes of stars, moons, and planets circled her earlobes and cascaded to her shoulders. She'd twisted her dreadlocks into a volcano-shaped cone rising from her skull. Satin ribbons flowed from the cone like lava. It occurred to me that I might have been better off spending Glen's money on a cab and a load of laundry. Maybe jeans and a T-shirt wouldn't be that obvious.

Lilly interrupted my thoughts. "Here we are. Now let's hurry. We don't have much time, and we have a lot of work to do." She pulled up next to the eggplant, parked, and bolted from the car leaving a cloud of patchouli and the tinkling of bells in her wake.

After a shower, I sat on the edge of Lilly's bed and watched as she pulled clothes from closets, drawers, and boxes. She held up flowing dresses, spangled tunics, and even a lavender-colored tutu. Although we were about the same size, I could not imagine myself in any of her clothing—even for a costume party. I held my breath and crossed my fingers. Time was running out. I might have to wear dirty jeans after all, or maybe come up with an airtight reason why I absolutely could not attend the millionaire's party.

One by one, Lilly held up, evaluated, and rejected pieces until finally, she made a selection.

"Perfect," she said. "Now, let's deal with your hair and get you dressed."

Lilly's black heels were a half size too big for me. "No worries," she said, "we'll crumple paper and stuff it into the toes. It will work. Trust me." She grabbed a piece of paper from a stack of mail on her counter. Before she mangled it, I noticed the shoe-stuffing material was a bill from Puget Sound Electric. I grinned. Lilly might be dressing me, but clearly, she was picking up a thing or two from my playbook.

At Lilly's insistence, I practiced walking around the Quonset hut in the heels for a few minutes to get the hang of it. Except for a muffled crunching sound— electric bills aren't that easy to crumple—I did pretty well. With Glen's forty bucks still intact, and squirreled away in my bra, I was ready to party.

When we arrived at Winslow's estate, Lilly waved off the valet and dropped me at the front door. I'd made it past the butler, moved down a long hall to the dining room, piled a china plate with appetizers, had managed to score a second glass of wine, and was in mid-bite on a spicy little sausage when an elegant, icy-looking woman approached me. I imagined that her dress—black satin embroidered with burnished gold threads—probably cost more than my car when it was new. And I was quite sure that the single gem resting in the hollow of her throat would fetch twice the asking price if I were ever to put *Ink Spot* on the market.

"You must be that girl from the insurance company. Right?" She started to hold out her hand, then withdrew it when she appeared to notice that I was packing a plate in one hand and a glass in the other.

I didn't like being called "that girl," and her smirk made me cringe, but all I could do was nod and swallow.

She looked me up and down, and I swear, she sniffed. "Your boss assures me that you are almost finished with your investigation. I'm pleased to hear that as I've held up my construction team too long already."

Okay, now I knew who she was. Elaine Dupont. I couldn't quite figure out why she was here, at Winslow's party, although it was clear she was wealthy, and the wealthy hang together. She cut me off before I could speak. Her eyes narrowed—she took one step closer and spoke in a tone too low for anyone but me to hear.

"I understand that you have plans to do some sailing when this job—when my report—is done. Perhaps that sailing trip of yours could happen in the near future. The very near future. You should know that I'm always happy to reward those who do an especially good job for me. Do keep that in mind." She gave me a smile that sent a cold shiver down my spine, as she turned and melted into a sea of black silk and diamonds.

My appetite disappeared and I felt a little sick. As much as I hated to abandon free food, I left the plate on the buffet table and wandered toward the front door. I intended to pound down the wine—couldn't let that go to waste—and then head for home. City Wide had attended and been seen—my job here was done. I'd get one of the valets to call a cab. That was my plan before I took a wrong turn and ended up in a long hallway. Might as well explore the place, I thought. Will probably never be in digs like this again, at least not in this lifetime.

I wandered along, pushed doors open, poked my head into several rooms, and marveled at the art and expensive, gilded furniture. French. Baroque, maybe.

Over-the-top in my opinion, but hey, somebody's gotta keep those gold-leafing guys in business. At the end of the hall, I noticed an open door—an invitation to explore, for sure.

With its walls of dark polished teak, massive walnut desk, and a gallery of framed boating photos, the room introduced itself as Winslow's home office. Couldn't be anything else. Sailing trophies lined the shelves of a glass-doored cabinet. As with his workspace downtown, huge windows framed views of the water, and here, the scenes also included lush, meticulous landscaping. The room smelled of oiled leather and money. Maybe because of all the boating images or because of the lack of gaudy gold cherubs, I relaxed. I slipped out of Lilly's shoes, let my feet rest on the thick Oriental rug, and moved to the wall to study the photographs.

Many of the shots recorded races in progress, while others showed winners with their arms and trophies raised in victory. There were several photos of dignitaries and celebrities and even one with a US president all standing and smiling with Port Commissioner Lawrence Winslow. There was also a smattering of more personal, more intimate images. Most of these were sepia-toned rather than the stark black-and-white of the racing shots. I recognized one of them immediately. I'd seen it before—in Charlie's room. A photograph of six friends smiling twenty-something smiles, their arms looped around each other, hands flashing peace symbols. Another photo showed a thin, awkward-appearing young man with a camera slung from a strap around his neck. His arm wrapped tight around the waist of a young woman with long, wild hair. The boy gazed at her with obvious adoration. The girl looked directly at the camera with a defiant grin. I glanced at the group shot and back to this one. Lawrence and Shirley—no question. Lost in my thoughts, I didn't hear him enter the room.

"Ah, Ms. Blue. Sheaffer. You did make it." He cleared his throat. "And by the way, I'd like to add, you look charming."

I spun around in time to see Lawrence Winslow appraising me. Busted. Despite my embarrassment, I felt a brief moment of pride. Lilly's choice for me—a black pencil skirt and conservative, yet soft, silk blouse in pale peach did add a little something missing from my everyday jeans and T-shirt look. "Oh, Commis...um, Larry. Hi. I hope it's okay—your office. I was looking at the sailing photos, and you know..." I rushed and stumbled through my sentences. "Hope I didn't..."

Lawrence smiled. "Not at all. I'm glad you could come. And I'm delighted you're interested in my work." He walked across the room and stood next to me. "Allow me to show you around."

Transferring his wineglass to his left hand, he used his right to make a sweeping motion toward the wall. "This is my sanctuary," he said. He gazed at the photos a moment, let his eyes travel slowly over the various images. "Well, at least they are the fruits of my sanctuary."

I must have looked confused because he went on to explain.

"As I mentioned when we first met, I've been developing black-and-whites since college—late high school to be more accurate. The photos in my office at work

are meant for the public, but these—these are special."
He touched a frame housing a photo of a sleek catama-
ran gliding over frothing waves—sails filled to the
spilling point. He seemed to retreat within, to go someplace far away and private.

I took a sip of wine and waited. After a few quiet
moments, Lawrence turned to me and smiled softly.
Genuine, I thought. First genuine emotion he'd shared
with me. Interesting.

Out loud, I said, "I didn't think anyone developed
photos anymore. Not with digital so cheap and easy."

He nodded. "True. It's a lost art. Or at least it's on the
endangered list. I find it relaxing and calming. Just me
and the trays in low, red light. And the images. The
images come to life right before my eyes. It's like
watching a birth." He shifted slightly. "Sadly, my wife
doesn't care for it. To be honest, she hates my hobby.
She says the chemicals stink and she's sure they're dangerous. She says she's allergic to them." He sighed. "But
she's allergic to everything. Carries one of those
EpiPens with her everywhere—even to formal dinners.
I think it's all in her mind."

He shook his head and straightened. His look
changed, and I knew he was back to his public persona,
or at least his lecherous old man persona. He took a
step closer, one step too close for my comfort. His
wine-scented breath was warm and moist. He leaned
toward me. "I could use a partner down there, in the
darkroom. Someone who knows about sailing and might
like to learn about photography. I could teach you…"

He took one more step and tripped over Lilly's shoes. His expensive, dark red wine splashed across the front of my borrowed blouse. What is it about men, and me, and spilled booze?

"Oh my God, I'm so sorry." Lawrence pulled the handkerchief from his blazer pocket, shook out the folds and then, in a slapstick comedic cliché, began to mop at the stain that soaked into the silk and spread over my breasts.

So, there we were, me barefoot, wearing a blousy equivalent of a wet T-shirt, and millionaire Lawrence Winslow, running his handkerchief—and hands—over my chest, while red wine dripped onto a priceless handwoven rug. That's when I heard the screech.

"Lawrence! What are you doing? Stop touching that woman!"

I don't know how long she had been watching our little comedy routine, but it couldn't have been long, because she certainly didn't see the humor in it. While the two of them flung choice words at each other, my brain whirled. I'd seen this woman before, and not only in the photo on Lawrence's desk downtown—it was more recent. I snapped my fingers. They both stopped mid-word.

"I know who you remind me of," I said. "You look just like Elaine Dupont!" I stood there, in my wine-wet blouse grinning stupidly at the port commissioner and his gorgeous, and furious, trophy wife.

"I should look like her," she hissed. "She's my mother."

# 20

Before I even figured out how it happened, I was whisked into the back of a cab. I wore a dry polo shirt with a Seattle Yacht Club logo embroidered on the pocket and held a plastic bag containing Lilly's shoes and her wet blouse. The cab driver had been paid and knew the shortest way to my marina. None of this seemed quite right to me—but I guess it's true, the rich live in a different world for sure.

The driver yielded to a bit of light flirting and stopped at the deli long enough for me to grab a small bottle of JD, a loaf of bread, and a jar of chunky peanut butter. After some quick addition, I figured I had enough cash left for one can of cheap cat food. The twenties were damp as the wine had soaked through my bra, but the kid at the checkout counter didn't appear to care. He seemed to enjoy watching me fish around for the bills. I was thirty cents short. He grinned and told me he'd cover it.

After feeding the cat, I filled my galley basin with cold water, added a squirt of shampoo, and submerged Lilly's blouse with the hope that if I left it overnight, the suds would remove the wine stain. I lit one small candle, flicked the rest of the lights off, and slipped into a pair of sloppy sweatpants and a baggy cotton sweater. Snuggled against the back of my port settee with my feet tucked under me and the cat at my side, I sipped my favorite whiskey from a coffee mug. Ah, the end of a long and hectic day, and now, for a while, peace and quiet. Except for the fact that Chen hadn't answered any of my calls or texts, life was pretty good.

"You should have seen the look on her face," I told the cat. "There was her husband more or less feeling me up and me, standing there, barefoot, holding a glass of wine." I laughed out loud. The cat looked up and made a low, gurgling sound in the back of his throat. He turned his attention to grooming one of his tufts of fur—the one that was growing back in a patch the shape of Florida. "You know," I continued to talk to the critter, "this whole thing is a little too weird for me. First, there's your person, Shirley, burned to a crisp. And come to find out, she was the college lover of Lawrence Winslow, now one of Seattle's port commissioners. And would you believe it, he's married to Elaine Dupont's daughter. And Elaine Dupont's father was recently found all snug in his cement grave in the I-90 Bridge. Too many things tied together to be coincidences." I stroked the cat's bristle-covered head. A low rumbling rewarded me. "I bet Chen has this figured out already and I bet he's holding out on me."

Thinking of Chen made me feel both sad and irritated. Sad because, well...why? What did I care if some random, uptight police detective had missed out on one of the best nights of his life? Irritated because the least he could do was answer my text—who does he think he is? What makes him think he's so special?—I must have been more agitated than I realized, because I petted the cat too hard. He stood up, jumped down, and crossed to the other side of the salon. He hopped up on the starboard settee, stretched, turned around twice, and plopped down, and then, after glaring at me for a moment, yawned and lowered his head to his paws.

As I finished my drink, I thought and fumed about Chen. Then the phone rang. It was Spiderman wanting to know if he could he come by and play? I thought for a moment. Since I'd last rolled around with him I'd seen a dead body, been doused twice with cold booze, had my boat and my car impounded—at least the boat was now free—had hobnobbed with folks way out of my demographic group, and had been rejected by a guy I didn't even care about.

"Sure," I told him, "come on by. The main gate is broken, so let yourself in. And, by the way, bring a bottle of Jack. You drank all of mine the last time you were here."

I hung up, hopped off the settee, hid my bottle, and headed for the V-berth for a change of clothes. I wanted to slip into something more appealing—cutoffs or something—before the surfer guy arrived.

For a split second, I wondered, again, if Spiderman had sprung for the release of my boat, but again, I dismissed the thought. Like me, his paycheck evaporated before it was cashed and besides, I didn't think he had the brain cells to figure out how to pay off someone else's bills. We didn't have much in common, Spider-man and me. It would be sex—just good, old-fashioned, wild, and probably drunken, sex. I flashed on the image of Chen as he'd leaned in close enough for a kiss. I stopped myself. I didn't need complications, and Chen was complicated. I pushed him out of my mind. Good sex—exactly what I needed to reset my emotions and clear my brain. Good, old-fashioned, drunken sex.

Sunlight spiked through the overhead hatch and woke me. I didn't need to roll over to look at my companion—I knew I'd find an inviting and sensuous man all wrapped up in baby-boy appeal. Tousled blond hair, one arm probably slung over his eyes, pouty lips blowing little spit bubbles as he sighed in his sleep. I didn't need to lean in close to breathe the thick, musky smell of everything we'd shared—our scent hung pungent in the warm, moist air of my cabin. Another faint scent lingered as well—cigarette smoke. I didn't remember him smoking last night but then...there was probably quite a lot I didn't remember from last night. No matter. I felt achy in that hurts-so-good sort of way. I considered waking him for another round, a sleepy, snuggly morning round. But first, I needed to pee.

We'd gone through most of his whiskey, and after that, we chased it with the beers Chen had left behind. I clenched at the thought of Chen and immediately wondered if he'd responded to my text. Now, more than the need to empty my bladder, or to sate my libido, I needed to satisfy my curiosity. I slid off the bunk and moved into the salon for my clothes.

Seattle's sky was crystal-clear, the temperature already warm enough for shorts and a tee, and although it was slightly past nine, the wooden dock felt hot on my bare feet. On the way to the marina's bathroom, I scrolled through my phone, scanning texts, emails, and the numbers on recent voice messages. A neighbor hoisted a coffee mug in greeting as I passed his boat, another looked up from her deck-painting project and smiled at me. I should have been happy. I'd survived a cocktail party with the rich and famous, with the only real faux pas executed by the host. Plus, I'd spent several delightful hours rolling in the sheets with a guy who...well, let's just say, the boy had his skills. But the truth was, I felt deflated, disappointed, and a little depressed. Over thirty messages landed in my phone while I'd been spinning with Spiderman and not one of them from Chen. Shouldn't have mattered. Somehow, it did.

A half hour later I wrapped my hands around a warm coffee mug and watched my young lover lope up the dock. A good-looking kid, I thought—tall, tanned, and while a bit awkward, even gangly on land, he was sure-footed on a surfboard and completely confident beneath a headboard. He turned, gave a loose wave and a goofy grin. I smiled and waved back.

No doubt about it, like so many young guys, Spiderman was sweet and sexy and a lot of fun, but somewhere along the line, you have to roll over and talk to them. And that's where it all breaks down. I was pretty sure that this time would be the last time with my surfer boy from Ballard. I felt bad about his most recent tattoo—an old-fashioned ink bottle labeled Schafer. I hadn't had the heart to tell him about the permanent misspelling of both my name and the name of the iconic ink manufacturer. It wasn't that important, probably no one else would ever notice, and besides, it was time for me to move on. I didn't have a clue who or even what was coming next, yet I knew this ride had come to an end. I sighed and took a sip of coffee. Stale, instant coffee. I'd found the jar behind a tube of K-Y Jelly in the galley cabinet—don't ask. It tasted horrible. Still, caffeine was caffeine.

The cat padded across the cockpit, jumped up on the bench, and stood next to me sniffing the air. It was almost as if he wanted to go for a morning sail. "Sorry, buddy." I touched one finger to his nose. "I have to work today. Hold that thought, though."

I knew the clown would be dying to know what had happened at that party and I needed to figure out how to word the story. I stood, stretched, and spoke again to the cat. "Don't worry; it won't be long now. This incident will be cleaned up and then you and me, we're going to untie and take off for Mexico. They're loose on the rules and regulations about animals down there. We'll get you into the country no problem. You can spend your days chasing geckos, your nights hunting cockroaches."

As promising as I hoped that sounded, I'm not sure the cat believed me. He arched his back, stuck his butt in the air, flicked his tail, and strolled to the stern without giving me another glance.

# 21

The phone rang, or rather, the phone played circus music.

"Sheaffer, car trouble. I'm waiting for AAA and a tow. Can you manage the office without me?"

After offering him several reassuring lines, we hung up. That man was such a dimwit—no way was I going to sit in that dreary office on a gorgeous summer day. Now, with the gift of free time, I considered my options. My first thought, of course, was to untie and get on the water. Take *Ink Spot* out through the Ballard Locks, spend the entire day zigzagging in the wind. I spent several minutes thinking about a nice long sail. Then, I remembered all the unfinished projects on my old boat. I could spend the day fixing things which would mean a day of begging and cajoling the guys at West Marine into giving me an IOU for necessary parts. A wink and a nudge should work.

On the other hand, I didn't have much to report on the current case, and to tell the truth, my curiosity was piqued. There had to be more clues hiding on Dock W— clues I was sure I could find if I poked around enough. Maybe the guard cops would be gone by now, and if not, I'd figure out a way to get past them. Again, a wink and a nudge.

*Okay, Blue*, I reasoned with myself. *Why not have it all? Take the cat out sailing for a few hours, then head on over to Dock W and spend some time looking around Shirley's houseboat.* On the way home, I could stop off at the chandlery and pick up a kit to fix the toilet. It would be nice to be able to pee onboard—much more convenient than walking up the dock every time I needed to recycle a bottle of beer.

Decision made, I spent a half hour or so checking fluids, pressing on tubes, testing the hold of clamp screws, and sitting there in the cramped doorway of the engine room listening to my old Perkins 4108 as it warmed up. Some of my gal-pals tell me that I'm missing a lot by not having children. They say there is nothing quite like caring for a small human as it grows. That may be true, but I think they're missing out by not caring for a big diesel engine. In my mind, there is nothing quite as satisfying as knowing all the parts, and all the functions of a powerful machine.

When I felt confident that my engine was warmed and ready, I hopped up on deck, pulled the sail cover off the main, stashed it below, and untied. The cat and I were off for an adventure.

Vessels crowded the narrow channels while tourists swarmed the viewing stands above the Ballard Locks. Cell phones and video cameras pointed at *Ink Spot's* deck to the cat who'd placed himself at the center of attention. I had to laugh. His fur was growing in and his entire body looked like a giant chin with three-day stubble. Still, he sat on the bow, proud and regal, soaking in veneration from his adoring admirers.

We spent most of the day catching the wind, tacking, then catching the wind for a ride in the opposite direction. I practiced difficult boat-handling moves for the fun and challenge, while the cat wedged himself in a corner on the port side and bathed in the sun. Yep, I decided, that critter was permanent crew.

By four I felt strong, rested, and ready to head on home. There were still several hours before sunset—enough time to get through the locks, motor into the slip, secure the boat, and head on over to Dock W before dark. Maybe even figure out some way to grab a bite as it occurred to me that I hadn't had anything all day except that instant coffee over eight hours ago. Because I'd used all of Glen's money, I decided to hang around in the parking lot until someone offered me a ride. City marinas are busy with boaters coming and going. They are usually on their way to buy parts for broken boats, and they're almost always generous and friendly. When I have money or gas, I share it. When I need money or gas, someone helps me out. It wasn't even a full ten minutes before my neighbor, Janis, two slips down, offered me a lift.

"So, what's broken on your boat?" I offered the standard mariner greeting as I slid into her aging Ford pickup.

Janis laughed. "Weirdly enough, nothing at the moment. Knock on wood—hate to say that out loud. You know, gremlins." She tapped her skull and smiled. "Nope, no boat problems at the moment. I'm on the way to the airport to pick up my new fellow. He's flying in from Oakland. Can't wait." She glanced at me for a reaction.

I could tell she was itching to share the news about this new guy so I asked, and she let loose. She told me all about how they met, the things they had in common, how his eyes lit up when he smiled. She glowed and sighed and giggled—literally giggled—and went on and on about all that gooey stuff women talk about during the first few weeks of a new relationship. I knew the story would change. I suspected that in the next month or so we'd be sharing a bottle of wine and she'd either be crying or plotting revenge. Now, though, she was happy, and I was pleased for her. For a moment, I almost felt sorry for myself, and then, I flashed on the freedom I'd felt standing behind the helm of my boat. Free and alone. Alone and free.

When we arrived at Dock W's gate, I swiveled around to give her a big hug and bumped the knob on the radio—news headlines blasted through the speakers.

"And in local news, King 5 has learned that the officer shot last night was released from Harbor View with only minor injuries. There is a full police investigation underway, although there is still no indication who the shooter is. The mayor of..."

I didn't hear the rest of the newscast. I must have stiffened when I heard the words "officer shot," because Janis drew back from our hug, and, still holding onto my shoulder, she searched my face.

"Blue, are you okay?"

"Oh yeah, of course." I gave her another squeeze, pulled away, and opened the truck's door. "I know a bunch of guys on the police force. Bummer to hear someone got shot, that's all. Sounds like a flesh wound, so that's good. Now you," I smiled wide, "you have yourself an amazing time with your new guy. And take good notes. I want to hear all about it!"

Soft, low light cast long gray shadows against the wooden slats of Dock W. The place seemed deserted—no yapping dogs, no skateboarding boys, not even a single lavender-haired old lady. The only sounds came from a single floatplane circling to roost for the night and the faint tinkle of a cell phone somewhere back in the parking lot. Good, I told myself, easier to sneak into Shirley's houseboat with no one around. Piece of cake. Still, for some reason, I felt a little uneasy, as if I were being watched. To make fun of myself, I hummed the theme song from a recent zombie/slasher movie. It didn't help.

There were no guards at Shirley's houseboat, only several lengths of limp crime-scene tape secured the door and windows. I stepped on the deck, pushed the broken screen and the door aside, ducked under the tape, and entered. I half expected to feel afraid or creeped out when I closed the door—instead, a sadness settled around my shoulders. Sadness and some embarrassment.

It was clear that someone, I suspected a team of investigators, had already gone through Shirley's belongings. It occurred to me that if a team of professionals couldn't figure anything out, what was a poser like me going to find? I sighed. It had seemed like a good idea this morning. Oh well, I thought, I'm here now—might as well make the best of things while there's still light.

I stood in the middle of Shirley's living room and scanned its contents with what I hoped was the deep intensity all professional investigators use. Who was I kidding—that was probably not going to happen— probably not ever. So, after a few minutes of failure, I took a different approach. If I were sitting in low, evening light in *Ink Spot's* cabin with a cup of tea, or more likely, a bottle of beer, and I let my eyes wander around my small messy home, what would I see? I filtered out the fire damage, blocked out the acidic smell permeating the building, and allowed my eyes to drift unhurriedly over furniture, knickknacks, and art. I lingered on surfaces—bookshelves, a tabletop, walls. Something was different. Something was missing.

On one wall, three dark patches marked the spots where frames had hung for a long time—long enough for the wallpaper around them to fade to several shades lighter. One patch filled the size of an eight-by-ten frame hung horizontally. Another was square and the third an oval shape. I thought it was strange that I hadn't noticed these marks the first time I'd been here and I wondered if Chen had. Chen. My fingers itched to reach in my pocket and check my phone for texts. I bit my lip and forced myself to push onward.

Careful to avoid stepping on anything, I moved through the debris on the floor, and gently toed a jumble of material at the base of the wall until I found the frames. I decided that they must have fallen during the fire—maybe dislodged by the force of the fire crew beating on the door with their axes.

Shattered glass in the oval frame had once protected the piece of white linen now damp and stained tea brown. I was familiar with the embroidered Walt Whitman quote, "This is what you shall do. Love the earth and sun and the animals."

Although one edge of the wooden frame had cracked and splintered, the square of glass remained intact. The damaged piece held a faded black and white photo of three young women in bathing suits, playing on a sunlit beach, forever bonded in vampish poses, laughter, and the happy companionship of good friends. I peered down at the picture and wondered which one was Shirley and if the other two were Geraldine and Dorothy. I flashed on the many selfies Lilly and I had taken over the years and wondered if our digital smiles would last as long as these paper grins.

Finally, I searched for the eight-by-ten frame. I turned over a couple of soaked magazines, pushed a scorched throw pillow to one side, and eased down to the bare floor, still careful to not crush anything under my feet or knees. No sign of the frame, no indication of what it held. That seemed odd, so I decided to review the shots I'd downloaded to the office computer. If the frames had been in place the first morning I'd been here, I'd know two things—first, what message or image the missing one held, and second, that someone else had been through here since then. Chen had ordered guards and police tape to secure the scene. Could have been some neighbor who snuck in for a peek at the destruction and found something he, or she, liked. Or, maybe, the missing frame held something that someone didn't want anyone else to see. My nerves tingled. There I was, acting and thinking like a *real* investigator. I could take this to Chen, impress the hell out of him. That would show him who "stumbled over" clues. Feeling elated and completely full of myself, I stood and edged through the debris until I reached the back entrance. I pushed it open and stepped onto the rear deck.

The temperature had dropped from late afternoon warm to that pleasant evening chill that calls for a favorite sweater or a lover's embrace. I shivered, rubbed my arms and breathed in the fishy scent of the lake and the sweet fragrance of the honeysuckle and night-blooming jasmine that wound through a trellis on the floating home next door. From across the lake, a woman's laugh traveled high and light, a dog barked, and a dinghy's motor putt-putted toward home. Heavy sigh— it was time for me to go home, too.

A peanut butter sandwich and a shot of whiskey called. And, I figured my new crew member would also be starving about now. Besides, there was nothing left to do here. As I turned toward the door, I glanced down and something white caught my eye. The pointed end of a small boat was wedged tight and partly submerged under Shirley's houseboat. Any thoughts of food, or whiskey, or even the cat, vanished. The triangle of white fiberglass had my full attention. I dropped to my knees and hung over the edge of Shirley's deck. Even in the dim light, I could tell that it was a fiberglass dinghy—probably a Walker Bay—the kind you can row and also sail. I could imagine Shirley and her cat tooling around the lake on calm evenings.

Grinning, I reached under the deck to grab the line looped through the ring in the boat's bow and gave a tug. The vessel would not budge. I tried again. No movement. I continued to lean over the deck as I considered the issue.

I knew these little boats. I knew that foam filled their seats and that even when full of water, they wouldn't sink. This one had probably drifted under, and out from under, Shirley's houseboat with waves from the wake of passing vessels several times a day. That is, before the fire. I reasoned that water from the fire hoses must have filled the dinghy, causing it to ride low and, that the extra weight of the soaked building and its contents had weighted the little boat down and wedged it in place. It occurred to me that although the houseboat was a total loss, the dinghy might be salvaged. I was so involved in figuring out how to deal with the situation that I didn't hear what had to have been footsteps. Even stranger, I didn't feel a shifting of the houseboat when someone stepped aboard. The only thing I remember was a hard kick to my butt. I plunged headfirst into the shockingly cold lake.

My first reaction was disorientation, my next, panic. I twisted into a ball and then somersaulted toward the surface. Before I could emerge, a hand pushed on my head and held me down. I flailed and scissor-kicked. Then, in a flash of clarity, I dropped below the hand, used my arms to push myself down further, and took two strokes toward the houseboat. I can usually hold my breath for quite a while—practice from cleaning the bottom of *Ink Spot*—but this time I'd gone in so fast, I didn't have a chance to grab a deep breath. My lungs were about to burst when I popped up, under the houseboat, next to the dinghy. There was about a foot of space between the bottom of Shirley's houseboat and the surface of the lake. Just enough room for me to hold my face out of the water. I gasped for air. Then, I yelled.

"Help! Somebody, help!"

The structure above me rocked, and I looked up in time to see the entire building lift and then drop. A floor-beam smacked my forehead. "Shit." That hurt and I knew it would leave a bruise. The dinghy pitched sideways and slammed into my shoulder. I dipped down to avoid another conk on the head and got a mouth full of lake water. I spit it out, grabbed the edge of the dinghy, and hung on. I yelled louder.

"Help! Help!"

Whoever had been on the houseboat must have left because now the structure barely moved. I clung to the partly submerged dinghy, shivered in the frigid water, gulped musky air, and yelled as loud as I could. My head throbbed, and my fingers cramped around the slippery fiberglass.

Although it felt like hours, I'm sure it was only minutes until I heard the clatter of footsteps, the jangle of voices, and the scrabble and scratching of tiny toenails on wood. My first thought was rats. Christ, rats! But then the yelping and yapping of a kennel full of canines announced the arrival of the renter living on the houseboat with the rainbow-colored flag.

"Here! Grab my hand."

All I could see through the darkness under Shirley's houseboat was an arm stretched toward the lake's surface and the blurry shadows of five small dogs racing back and forth at the edge of the dock.

To reach safety, I had to dog-paddle to the back of Shirley's deck and then maneuver around her home and between it and the neighboring houseboat. Lake Union doesn't get warm, even in the summer. I was so cold I could barely move my legs to navigate through the tangle of underwater tubing and lines that hindered my progress. When I made it to the edge of the dock and felt that tight grasp of help, a final shot of energy surged through me. I scrambled up, flopped over on my back, and gulped fresh air. Tiny tongues immediately went to work lapping the lake from my face.

Dorothy, along with several other neighbors crowded around. With the older woman's help, I sat up on the wooden dock, cross-legged and dripping. Geraldine wrapped a blanket around my shoulders as the little dogs jumped on me and licked my arms and legs. I shivered, dropped my head, and closed my eyes.

Dorothy leaned over and patted my back. "Don't worry dear. You're safe now. We're here with you. You take a minute to catch your breath, then we'll get you to my house and into some warm, dry clothes."

"We'll take care of you," Geraldine added.

True to their words, the ladies did take care of me. They introduced me to their neighbor, Desmond, the man who'd pulled me from the lake. Desmond lived in the houseboat with the stained-glass windows and the rainbow flag. He introduced his little dogs—each named after an American president. While I was getting to know Milhous, Gerry, Jimmy, Ronny, and Clint, Bud had arrived bearing a bag of pretzels, a can of Pringles, and a box of wine. Dorothy heated tomato soup and warmed up leftover meatballs.

While I showered, Geraldine took my wet clothes to her house for a wash and dry. These neighbors—all strangers to me a week ago—were pitching together to do whatever it took to keep me warm, and dry, and safe. I felt loved—not something I'm used to. I stood under the hot water and felt my heart expand.

Dorothy's tiny bathroom was thick with steam when I stepped out of the shower, so it took me a moment to focus on the dry clothing she'd laid out for me. A pair of lilac granny panties with a matching camisole, a button-down dress covered with red and yellow butterflies, and a pair of fuzzy yellow socks. I towel-dried my hair, dressed, and stepped into Dorothy's now crowded living room. The neighbors passed around pretzels and chips and drank cheap red wine from jelly jars. Desmond's five dogs lay in a neat row, each gnawing on a small rawhide bone.

"Oh, there you are dear," Dorothy sat her wine on a table and walked over to me carrying a brown wool shawl. She draped it over my shoulders and offered the choice of a cup of cocoa or a jar of wine. I went for the warmth of the cocoa.

"Well, of course, we're all dying to know what happened to you. We know that you fell in but how did you get that giant goose egg?" Desmond peered at my forehead. "That has to hurt."

The others leaned in and waited as I settled into an overstuffed chair. I reached up and touched the spot where my forehead had whacked against the bottom of Shirley's houseboat. Desmond wasn't exaggerating—the bruise *was* the size of a goose egg.

"I don't know what happened, exactly. I was leaning over the deck to look at Shirley's dinghy and..."

Three sharp knocks on the door startled me. All five of the dogs looked up. Jimmy, or maybe it was Milhous, growled low in his throat.

"Oh, my. I almost forgot." Dorothy pushed to standing and hurried to the door. "That will be your young man. We called him when you were in the shower. We knew you'd want to be with him at a time like this."

*My young man? What young man?* So, there I was, with wet hair, wearing a calf-length house dress, fuzzy yellow socks, and an old woolen shawl, when Dorothy welcomed Detective David Chen into her home.

# 22

Chen took a moment—stood in the doorway—scanned the room until our eyes met. He took three steps, stopped in front of my chair, and leaned over so close I could smell his cologne, so close I could feel his panic.

"Ms. Blue. Are you okay? What happened? What were you doing in that place, in the dark, alone? You could have been seriously injured. Why didn't you call me?"

His words and obvious concern tumbled out so fast he didn't seem to filter them—didn't seem to even think about what he was saying. He must have noticed my slight grin and the raised eyebrows of Bud and Dorothy, because in a flash he stopped, flushed, and straightened. It was then I noticed that his jacket hung loosely over his shoulders and that his left arm was held snug against his chest by a dark-colored sling. I tilted my head.

"And just what happened to *you*, Detective Chen?"

The moment would have been more awkward if Desmond hadn't cleared his throat and called to his dogs. "Come on boys, time for daddy to get going." He moved around Chen and gathered the five gooey raw-hide treats. Then he straightened and turned to me.

"Nice to meet you, Ms. Blue. Delighted to know the boys and I could be of help. Any time you need a hand up, you call us. Or come by to visit sometime, you know our door—the one with the rainbow flag." He glanced at the others. "Always a pleasure, my dear neighbors. Ta ta." He gave a curt bow, snapped his fingers, and turned toward the door. The little dogs followed behind, tails and butts wagging in unison.

"Well, now. Where are our manners?" Dorothy said. "Detective, what can we get you? Wine? Cocoa? Maybe a nice cup of coffee? Policemen like coffee, right?"

Chen shook his head no. "Thank you so much—very kind of you. However, I think I should get Ms. Blue here home. Or maybe get her to the emergency room so a doctor can look at that bump." He smiled at me. "Guessing you could use a ride?"

"Yeah," I mumbled. "But not to the hospital. I'm fine. I just wanna go home—to the marina—to my boat."

After friendly hugs, and a slew of advice directed to me, "stay warm, drink fluids, get rest," and after stern directions for Chen, "you take good care of her, don't let her out of your sight, make sure she eats," we managed to extract ourselves from the well-meaning folks on Dock W.

Chen held onto my arm all the way up the dock, up the rickety stairs, and across the lot to his car. I wasn't sure if he was trying to steady me, or himself. It didn't matter—I liked the touch.

I breathed in the scent of new car. The sleek BMW looked and felt expensive. Because Geraldine had forgotten to take my clothes—including my deck shoes—out of her washing machine, I still wore Dorothy's outfit minus the yellow socks. I wriggled my bare toes in the vehicle's thick carpeting and sank into the cushy front seat.

"Nice car." I brushed my hand over the polished wood console. "Guess Seattle PD pulled out all the stops for their exchange program."

Chen flicked the blinker. "No, the SPD maintains a fleet of unmarked beaters. This is a rental. My dime." He waited a moment and then turned to me. "You aren't going to agree to go to the hospital, are you?" He didn't even wait for my answer. Just shook his head and backed from the parking spot.

I must have been exhausted because I don't remember a thing—not even the sound of crunching gravel as Chen turned into the marina's parking lot, or the switch to silence when he cut the engine.

"Sheaffer. Wake up. You're home."

"Oh, wow." I struggled from my slumped position. My muscles had already begun to ache from my plunge into the lake. I reached for the door handle. "Hey, thanks for the ride and all. It was nice of you to come." I thought for a few seconds and then said, "Look, I know I owe you an explanation because, well, because we're supposed to be working on this together. So, I'm sorry I've been such a..." I paused before going on.

Chen didn't look at me. His left arm hung cradled in the sling, his right rested on the steering wheel. He stayed silent. I could tell he was listening.

"So, I think I might have discovered something that could be important. If you want, I can meet you at the station tomorrow and...you know, share my findings." I hoped I sounded more professional and less small and pathetic than I felt.

He lowered his hand from the wheel and turned toward me. "We did get off to a rough start. Still, to be honest, I don't think you should be alone—at least not for a while. That bump on your forehead is swelling—you could have a concussion. Probably not. But even so..." He paused and searched my face for a moment. When I didn't answer, he continued.

"My guess is that you're already starting to hurt because from what I gather, you suffered a bit of a bouncing around under that boat. A hot meal can work wonders. Why don't you get into your own clothes, feed the cat, and later I'll come back and pick you up. We can go for a quiet meal and discuss the case. We can share what we've learned—maybe make some headway. Sound good?" He stopped and waited.

I wanted to make it down to *Ink Spot,* to crash in my messy bunk, to forget this day even happened. At the same time, I wanted more. "Sure," I said, "sounds good."

As I padded down the dock, I thought about the past few hours, and about being pushed off the dock and held under water. Was someone trying to kill me? At first, the thought made me shiver and walk faster. By the time I reached my boat, I was more confused than frightened. Why would anyone want to kill me? It didn't make any sense. The only thing I could come up with was that whoever pushed me must have thought I was someone else. They had been trying to kill someone else, and I was just there. It wouldn't be the first time I'd been in the wrong place at the wrong time. I reached for the boarding ladder and winced. My muscles ached so much now I could barely climb the steps, and I almost reconsidered my decision to spend time with Chen. Then I thought about his arm in the sling. No doubt about it, he'd been the cop in the news report. Did someone shoot him? Could it be another case of wrong place, wrong time? He had more information about the case, and I had my observations about the missing frame. That, and the possibility that maybe someone *was* trying to kill me, or us, intrigued me. Plus, Detective Chen had offered a quiet time. That would mean time to learn more about the case, and maybe more about him, personally. I pushed through the pain.

Before Chen knocked on the hull, I'd fed the cat, changed into my cleanest pair of jeans and a long-sleeved tee, applied mascara, lipstick, and a hint of blush. I dabbed foundation on the bruise until I could barely see the discoloration and pulled my hair into what I hoped might be a French twist or at least a fancy ponytail. I even dabbed my wrists with dots of the essential rose oil Lilly had given me last Christmas.

He thumped on the hull three times. Stifling a groan, I climbed up the companionway and peered across the cockpit to the dock. Chen stood under a light, waiting. Something about the way he stood, all casual, and confident, something about the way he held his leather jacket over his shoulder with his free arm made me pause. He turned in time to catch me watching him and smiled.

"Be right there," I said. I eased back down the steps, patted the cat gently on the top of his bristly head, and took one swift swig of the strong Irish whiskey for courage. Now I was as ready as I would ever be for dinner with Detective David Chen.

We made small talk on the drive, nothing much. He asked about the cat and we laughed about the little dogs with their presidential names. We chatted about the weather—always a safe subject. Finally, he turned down a residential street at the base of Queen Anne Hill and pulled into a sloping drive in the front of a large, modern building at the edge of the hill—the posh side of Queen Anne Hill.

"This is where I'm staying," he said. "I thought a public restaurant wouldn't be the best place to discuss the case, so I threw some things together. Hope you like home cooking." With the click of a switch, a double garage door opened and Chen parked the Beemer.

He pressed an elevator button labeled PH, and we waited. I didn't put things together until we'd passed several floors and the elevator door opened directly onto an enormous room at the top of the building. Of course, PH—Penthouse. I stifled a gasp.

"Come on in," he said. "Relax. The prep work is almost finished, and it won't take long to heat things. I'll open a bottle of wine."

As he pulled the cork, I surveyed the large, open floor plan. One half housed a high-design kitchen. Copper pans hung from a cast iron rack, baskets of fresh fruit and crystal bowls filled with cut flowers punctuated black granite counters. Healthy broad-leafed plants and delicate orchards decorated tables and the top of a baby grand piano. Cushy furniture, upholstered in brocade and velvet, invited a relaxing and comfortable stay.

Glass panels with sliding doors offered a one-hundred-eighty-degree view of downtown Seattle.

Chen poured two glasses, then tapped a flat-screen twice. His first touch brought low, mellow jazz from unseen speakers, the second activated an indoor fountain. Water flowed over slabs of slate into a rock pond. I walked to the fountain and peered in. Twinkling lights lit the water from below and cast a silver glint on the scales of three fat koi which swam in lazy circles. Water lilies floated past a smiling Buddha that presided over the pond. All of this in one room. A room more lovely and peaceful than the entire gaudy mansion owned by Lawrence Winslow. I don't know much about wealth, or how the wealthy live, but I guessed this penthouse apartment was probably in the same price range as the Winslow Estate. And that made me uncomfortable—even more uncomfortable than I'd been during Winslow's cocktail party. Who was David Chen? If he was wealthy, why was he working in homicide? And, what the hell was I supposed to do with some rich guy? I felt way out of my league. I struggled to construct a reason to leave—to leave immediately.

Before I could come up with an excuse to bolt, Chen walked over and handed me a glass of red wine. I noticed that he still held his left arm close to his body, even though he'd removed the sling. I wanted to ask him about it but decided now wasn't the time. Also wanted to ask him how he got the limp, but it wasn't the time for that, either. So, I nodded, smiled, and looked back down at the pond.

"They're happy fish," he said. "But I might be over-feeding them because it's so relaxing to watch them go for the flakes of food."

"I thought you said pets are too messy for you."

"Oh, they're not mine. This place isn't mine. I'm house-sitting for..." He paused for a moment, stared down at the fish but didn't appear to focus on them. He seemed to struggle for the next words. "I'm house-sitting for a friend. She agreed to help me with a project back in San Francisco, and since I'm only here for a short time, I agreed to look after her apartment. It was perfect timing for both of us."

We stood side by side for a moment and watched the koi glide through lily stems. They cast shadows as they passed the lights recessed in the pond's walls. Once he'd moved beyond the part about his friend, Chen mellowed and he seemed at ease and comfortable—not at all pre-tentious or judgmental. His demeanor, and the facts that his car was a rental and this place a house-sitting gig, calmed my nerves. I was, of course, itching to find out more about this "friend," and his project back home, but I knew this wasn't the time—or probably the place. For the short term anyway, all was well. I exhaled.

He turned toward me and lifted his glass. "Toast?"

"Sure." I held my glass to his. "To what?"

"Colleagues," he said. "To working as colleagues."

Our glasses clinked, and as the smooth liquid slid down my throat, I lowered my eyes. Okay, colleagues. Chen saw us as colleagues. Good to know the game. And maybe this game wasn't so bad, and maybe Chen and I weren't so far apart. For a while there, I'd thought I might enjoy a little more than a working relationship...but hey, I could handle colleagues. That settled, I glanced up.

He was close. I looked into his eyes. All that stuff about colleagues? Poof. We stayed there for a long moment, and then, Chen took a half-step back.

"Hungry?" he asked.

We sat side by side on high stools at the kitchen bar, an arrangement casual enough to comfortably offset the upscale environment. I was famished and had a tough time not inhaling the meal, but that wouldn't have done justice to the home-cooking Chen had "thrown together." He'd prepared spinach ravioli filled with goat cheese and sun-dried tomatoes drizzled with a dark mushroom sauce. Baked asparagus spears brushed with olive oil and dotted with coarse sea salt complimented a Caesar salad tossed with poached salmon and artichoke hearts. What kind of guy cooks with artichoke hearts? A fragrant loaf of warm olive-bread nested in a basket covered with white linen and when he raised the linen, I glanced at his left hand. No ring. I sucked in a quick breath. No ring. Then again, he'd just been shot—maybe his fingers were swollen. Did I see a ring before? I almost always check for a ring immediately. Married men are an absolute no—no exception—no way. Too much hassle for my gig. Plus, I like my women friends, and women in general, too much to inflict unavoidable pain. I gave myself a swift mental kick for not finding out sooner.

"Sheaffer? Did you hear me?" Chen cleared his throat and tilted his head slightly as he asked the question. "I asked if you wanted more wine."

I know I flushed as I nodded. *Pay attention, Blue*—no more drifting—this is a business dinner. *A business dinner.*

As we ate, we shared what we'd learned about the case including what he'd gleaned from his second meeting with Lawrence Winslow.

"The guy is way too slick, too ready to be of help. I don't trust him." Chen dipped a piece of bread into a shallow dish of herbed oil. "What was your impression of the guy?"

I relayed what I'd learned during my first meeting with Winslow and how my impressions echoed Chen's. I did everything I could to appear externally cool and calm as if discussing a potential murder with a police detective was something I did every day. Inside I churned with excitement and nerves. This was the first time I could remember feeling—really feeling—that I was doing significant work. Even the *idea* of it thrilled me. If Chen noticed, he didn't let on.

We acknowledged that we'd both seen the dark, un-faded, spots on Shirley's wallpaper and since neither of us had reviewed the crime scene photos yet, we didn't know what the one missing frame held. Over a dessert of strawberries in cream and honey, I shared what had happened at Winslow's party and mulled over my ideas about the commissioner's darkroom hobby. I shared most of it anyway. I decided to leave out the part about getting a wine-wet shirt feel-up.

"Maybe Lawrence killed Shirley. His wife thinks the chemicals are poisonous. Didn't you tell me Shirley was poisoned?"

Chen nodded. "Poison, or something else. Something that caused her to drop before the fire even started. The coroner says he is certain she didn't die of smoke inhalation. That's all we know, so far. Winslow is hiding something. That's for sure." He picked up his glass.

"Well, we do know that Lawrence visited Shirley the day she died. We also know that around that same time a woman—a well-dressed woman—visited her. Could be Elaine Dupont because she was trying to get everyone to sell. Maybe she saw Shirley that day, too."

"How do you know that?" Chen stopped short of taking a sip of wine. "How do you know about a well-dressed woman visiting the victim that day?"

"The drawings," I said.

He straightened, sat his glass on the counter. His eyes narrowed, and his brow furrowed. "What drawings?"

I lowered my fork to the side of my plate. My hand shook. Maybe I was in over my head; maybe Chen had been premature in taking me on as "a colleague."

"What drawings?" he repeated.

I took a deep breath, released it and told him about Geraldine's art and how she recorded everything she saw, and how she'd kept paintings and sketches of her history—the history of the group of friends—for decades. I told him about the drawings of Lawrence Winslow and Shirley as young lovers, about the recent depiction of Lawrence walking away from the front door of Shirley's houseboat, and again, about the sketch of the well-dressed woman paying a visit. I left out the picture of yours truly and my dinner companion, embracing.

When I stopped, Chen seemed a bit deflated.

"Interesting," he said. "But nothing we can use." He sighed. "She's rattled. Shows signs of Alzheimer's or at least the beginning stages. We couldn't use her drawings. Too bad she didn't take up photography, like Winslow." He picked up his glass and took a sip.

Neither of us spoke for a few minutes. To change the tone, I asked about his arm.

"Gunshot," he said. "Someone took aim at me. Lousy shot, though; it's only a graze. Nicked the skin—that's all." He stretched his arm out a couple of times. "Doesn't hurt, really. A little sore, but no big deal."

"Do you think it was random? I mean, wrong place, wrong time sort of thing?"

He shook his head. "No. I don't."

"Well, why? Who? And if that's true, do you think the person who pushed me, who held me under, really knew it was me?" I felt light-headed.

Chen took a sip of wine, set his glass down, and turned to face me. "Here's my theory. I think Lawrence Winslow has something to do with this. And I think he's mixed up with the death of the commissioner found in the bridge. I'm quite certain Shirley had the key but, as you know, she's not going to give us any answers. That makes proving my theory harder."

I started to speak but he held up one hand.

"Let me add a little more," he said. "I believe that whoever shot me thinks I know more than I do. And I believe that same person also thinks you know more than you do. Right now, Winslow is on the top of my suspect list. I'm going to keep digging. All that, I get. What I *don't* get is this...I would think that someone like

Lawrence Winslow, with all that money, would try to buy you off, get you to stop poking around—reduce the number of eyes on him. But that hasn't happened, has it?"

My face felt hot, my throat dry. Had I been sitting on something important for days now? Had I completely bungled the process? I looked at Chen. He waited, his expression neutral.

"Well," I said, "maybe he did. Through Elaine Dupont. And maybe, on his own." Chen didn't respond. He simply continued to wait.

"At the party, Elaine offered me a bonus if I wrapped things up quickly. I didn't mention it earlier because, well, I didn't think about it much until now." As I spoke, I began to see that I *had* missed things. I wanted to bolt out of the place—hide in my boat with the companionway locked. But with no way out, I plowed on and forced myself to make eye contact with Chen. "And there was the thing about my boat. *Ink Spot* was detained due to a little uh...back rent issue. Someone paid—in full. I didn't dwell on who might have done that. I was just happy to have my boat free. Now I'm wondering if maybe Lawrence and Elaine are mixed up in this together in some way more than son-in-law and mother-in-law." I stopped talking. I felt embarrassed and inept. I'd been playing "investigator" without any knowledge of what I'd been doing, and I may have hindered the *real* investigation from moving forward. I looked down at my plate. "I should have told you when it happened. I'm sorry."

Chen reached over and put his hand on mine. "Sheaffer," he said.

I looked up, met his eyes.

"Don't worry about it. This is a puzzle. You added another piece. We're going to figure this out. That's my job. He gave my hand a light squeeze, then released it. With the topic clearly dismissed, Chen stood and stretched. "I'm going to clean up."

"Let me help." I started to stand.

"No. You relax. It won't take long. If you want, you might enjoy heading out to the deck. The view of the city at night is amazing."

I stayed seated for a bit and watched him as he rinsed our plates and slid them into the dishwasher rack. A simple housekeeping task, but somehow, he made it look important, and somehow, he made it look sexy. I flashed on the mountain of dishes in my galley and cringed as I thought about the many times I'd dipped a crusty plate into a salty wave on Puget Sound, swished it back and forth, given it a quick squirt of fresh water, and called it clean. There's nothing sexy about the way I did dishes. I cleared my throat and pushed the thought away.

"Ah, Chen...um, David, where is the head? I mean the restroom?"

He glanced up for a flash and nodded toward the hall. "First door on the left."

My entire aft cabin would have fit in his bathroom—with yards to spare. I stopped at the door for a moment and gaped at the black marble counters, gold-toned faucets, and the thick glass bowls that served as sinks. Collections of polished stones lay at the base of the bowls—something that made no sense to me. White orchid blossoms cascaded from stems tied to ebony chopsticks stuck in tall, gleaming black pots. I thought back to Lawrence Winslow's mansion as I scanned the room—the rich *really do* live differently.

I didn't need the facilities, but I did need time alone. I've had many meals with many men. This one was different. There was something unique about the spread I'd shared with David Chen, and it wasn't because it was, ostensibly, a business dinner. There wasn't anything particularly intriguing, just two people sitting on stools, eating pasta, and discussing crime. Chatting like colleagues, almost like friends. He hadn't done anything overt, no come-ons, no innuendos, and yet, there was something about the way he reassured me with one touch of his hand, and the way he did an everyday task—like loading a dishwasher—that sent my thoughts scurrying down a familiar rabbit hole. Most of the time, I slid down that path with eager anticipation yet, at the moment, my randy thoughts made me more uneasy than happy—more uncomfortable than titillated.

I've never been nervous or uptight about sex. It's a relatively simple formula if you think about it. Two or more pals—or strangers—get together and drink a lot, laugh a lot, tease and then, you slap the sheets. Easy. One of my cop buddies calls sex a game of slip and tickle—nothing heavy, just good, physical fun. That's always worked for me. So why did I feel like I was in a B-grade movie, with my hand on the knob of a door I knew I shouldn't open.

I leaned against the marble vanity, faced away from the mirror, and mentally chastised myself. *What's wrong with you, girl?* He hasn't made a move. Hasn't done anything that even seems like a move. You're jumping to conclusions. And besides, so what if he does? What's the big deal?

A splash of cold water helped cool my face. I touched the lump—it didn't look or feel any bigger now than it had been back on *Ink Spot* and the foundation continued to cover the bruise. I squeezed a line of Chen's toothpaste and finger-brushed my teeth. There. Much better. Back in control. I flicked the light off and marched down the hall.

He was leaning against the center kitchen island when I returned to the front room. He faced away from me, and I don't think he heard me enter—if he did, he didn't pay any attention. He nodded his head, and twirled one finger, obviously listening to some longish story.

"I know, honey." His words were soft, low, and soothing. "I miss you too. But this is work. Our new house isn't going to pay for itself. But it won't be much longer. I promise." He paused and listened again.

My stomach gripped into a tight clench. My mouth went dry, my tongue felt thick, and I couldn't swallow the lump that formed halfway down my throat. My entire body felt cold and numb despite being flushed just a few moments earlier. Clearly, in this case, no ring meant nothing.

"Yes, of course. That's a good idea. We can think about it together when I get home. Now, don't worry," he said. "I'm here for you, and everything is going to be okay." Chen stopped again—listened—nodded. "I love you, too." He touched the face of his phone and placed it on the counter as he turned around. When he saw me standing there, by the doorway, he smiled.

"Find everything you needed?"

What I needed was to get out of that penthouse and as far away from David Chen as possible—as quickly as possible. I spun out a plan in my mind—dash out the door, grab the elevator, get out to the main drag, hail a cab, get home, lock the companionway or better still, untie and sail away never to see Seattle or Detective David Chen again. A good plan except that the elevator needed a password—his password—and I had no cash for a cab, no cash for fuel for the boat, no cash for food for the cat, and no cash for food for me. Stuck.

Chen didn't reach detective level on his good looks— the guy was smart, and he knew people. He seemed to look right through me.

"What freaked you out? You look like you've just seen flashing red-and-whites in your rearview mirror."

Cop humor. But it wasn't funny—I did feel like I'd been busted, if only for having thoughts I wished I hadn't. I did my best to sound casual. "Oh no, I was just thinking how late it's getting and that I have to get to work early tomorrow and that I probably should be on my way...."

Chen narrowed his eyes, and I knew, he knew, I was lying about something. He just didn't know what, or why. "Well, we can get going soon if you'd like. But at least treat yourself to a quick look at one of Seattle's most beautiful night views before you leave. I have a couple of small things to wrap up in the kitchen, and then I'll join you."

I couldn't think of any way around it, so I took his suggestion and made my way onto the deck. Stretching across the entire roof and around the perimeter of the penthouse, the structure was the largest redwood deck I'd ever seen outside of a marina. Huge ceramic pots decorated with Chinese figures held bonsai trees, trailing vines, and flowers—some night-blooming and fragrant, some closed and resting until dawn. I leaned against the railing and gazed out over Seattle. The glittering city spread like a sequined gown flung over a king-sized bed. Elliot Bay, a black patent leather belt ribboned around the shoreline. One blazing white wedding cake of a ship—a cruise ship—pulled out on its way to Alaska or maybe to Mexico. I slumped. Mexico. I had hoped to earn enough money from this case to quit my job and sail away. Now, that dream seemed increasingly out of reach.

The glass door made a soft whoosh as Chen slid it open. I continued to look down at the twinkling lights and offered up a quick silent wish that he'd say he'd finished with the clean-up and was ready to drive me home. But he didn't do that. He walked across the deck without a sound and stopped close behind me. Although we didn't touch, I could feel the warmth of his body. I turned my head slightly, just enough for a quick peek at his profile. Chen seemed to focus on a spot far across the city, beyond the bay. I forced my gaze away from Chen and back to the glittering view and I tried my best to come up with some irreverent, wise-ass crack that would break the obvious tension and get me out of this miserable moment. But nothing—I had nothing. So, I stood there, in the lee of Chen's warmth, and waited. Finally, he sighed.

"I'm starting to fall for this city," he said. "If it weren't for my wife's parents living in Oakland, I'd pack up and move here permanently. But I think it's important for Willow to grow up close to family." He stepped from behind me and stood by my side. "She's had a rough go, and it wouldn't be right to add another loss by moving her away from her grandparents. Wouldn't be good for them either."

My pea-brain spun. Wife's parents? Willow? Another loss? "Willow is your daughter?"

"Yes. She'll be seven next month. She's a good kid. Smart. Happy. But I worry about her growing up with one parent in a flat in the center of San Francisco. She needs a home with a yard, some kids her own age to play with, and if you give her a chance, she'll tell you she 'really, really, really, really' needs a puppy." Chen surprised me as he imitated a petulant little girl begging for a pet.

I took a long shot. "I, um, heard you on the phone when I came out of the bathroom. Were you talking to your wife?"

Chen shook his head. "No, Joslyn has been dead for three years. It's just Willow and me, now." Then, without being asked, he added, "cancer."

"I'm sorry," I murmured.

He sighed again. "It's been pretty hard on both of us. But Joslyn's sister—this is her condo—helps out when I have to leave. And of course, the grandparents, they're a big help. Still, I know that Willow needs more than a puppy." He went silent for a moment, then excused himself. "I'll be right back."

As I waited for Chen to return, I did a mental rerun of the day because, to be honest, I was feeling a bit overwhelmed by the roller coaster ride of events and emotions. Especially emotions. Most especially the emotions around David Chen. I'd gone from mildly disliking him, to feeling irritated by his attitude, to overheating from a flush of lust, to experiencing a blood-draining chill and humiliation at the presumptuousness of my thoughts to now, what? Now, compassion.

The poor guy, a logical, tidy, gourmet cook, and lead detective, was doing his best to raise a little girl on his own. A little girl who pleaded for a puppy and maybe, I imagined, at times pleaded for a mommy as well. It had to be a difficult job.

I pushed my thoughts aside when Chen returned. He walked across the deck and stopped next to me.

"Brandy," he said. He handed me a heavy crystal snifter with a measure of the dark liquid. We tapped the snifters together, breathed in the sweet scent, and stood quietly, side by side. The warmth of the aged wine slid through me and melted any lingering tension.

We stayed there, in silence, in the peace of the night, for what seemed like ages. After a while, I realized Chen hadn't said a word since he'd handed me the brandy. I shifted and faced him.

"Whatcha thinking?" I asked.

He blinked once and turned toward me, now so close that even in the dim, ambient light, I could see flecks of gold in his eyes. "I'm wondering about you," he said.

"Moi?"

He ignored my glib response. "I'm interested, curious maybe, about you. About your name, Sheaffer Blue. I know it's the name of fountain pen ink bottled by the Sheaffer Company and that it's not in high demand these days. Why would anyone name a child after an out-of-date office product? Plus, the name of your boat, *Ink Spot*." He gave a quick shrug. "So, I know there's a story." He moved closer—so close that I caught the faint lingering scent of cream, honey, and warm wine on his breath—if he moved two more inches, our lips would touch. "Sheaffer Blue," he said my name low this time, "tell me your story."

"Later," I said. I heard my voice come out as a whisper. "I'll tell you later."

Chen nodded once. "All right. Later." Then he moved two inches.

We didn't romp, tease, slap or tickle. We caressed, and tasted, and breathed each other in. I felt his lips soft on my neck. I felt my back arch as a wave of electrical current spiraled up my spine. I think I called out.

"I've got you," he whispered. "You're safe. I've got you."

We lay still—let the beating slow, let the breathing lengthen, let muscles melt. When I finally shivered, Chen reached over and pulled the comforter up around my shoulders. I rolled to my side to look at him. He raised up on his good arm and smiled. A smile lit by the single candle still flickering on his nightstand.

"So," he said. He used one finger to push a damp strand of hair from my face. "It's later, Sheaffer Blue. Tell me your story."

I sat among a mound of pillows propped against the wooden headboard. While I waited for Chen to make cups of herbal tea, I looked around the room. I hadn't noticed it earlier, in fact, I didn't even remember moving from the deck to the bedroom and yet, here I was, in Detective David Chen's California king, about to spill what he called, "my story."

Like the rest of the penthouse, the bedroom's décor was uncluttered and pristine—gender neutral and expensive. A highboy, two nightstands, and a long dresser of polished bird's-eye maple matched the bedstead. Two wingbacks, upholstered in muted stripes faced each other across a low, round table. The now tousled bedding, decorative pillows, and accent touches were coordinated in colors my mother would probably call mauvy-taupe.

My mother. I sighed. She is one of the reasons I rarely talk about my background. In fact, except for Lilly, I don't think anyone knows the real story behind my name. The truth is, even though my name is a little weird, none of my buddies have ever seemed interested in it. Most people call me Blue, and well, maybe they assume that...I dunno what they assume. My thoughts were interrupted when Chen returned with two steaming cups. He appeared as comfortable serving tea in the bedroom wearing a black bathrobe as he'd seemed serving wine in the living room. He placed a coaster and cup on the nightstand next to me.

"This is chamomile," he said. "No caffeine, good for calming sore muscles and jangled nerves." He grinned. "But I trust your nerves are not jangled now, are they?" It wasn't a question.

I winked and gave his cheek a quick peck as he settled next to me.

"Okay," he said. "Storytime."

I blew across the hot tea, set it down, sighed, and started. "Well, you were right. Who names a child after office supplies? My mother, that's who. She's...well, she's special."

"Name?" Chen asked.

"Sylvia. No last name, just Sylvia. After the poet, Sylvia Plath. Her parents called her June Elizabeth, but when my mother was young, she attended some hippie-type school called the Jack Kerouac School of Disembodied Poetics. Evidently, it was a thing for students to drop their given names and adopt the name of a favorite writer. My mother loved Plath's *Tulips*, so she took the poet's name. My name was supposed to be Anne after Anne Waldman, another poet. However, as Sylvia describes it, things got a little crazy the night I was born."

Chen sat his cup down and changed his position so that he could face me. I'm never shy, but for some reason, I pulled the comforter up higher.

"Go on," he said. "I'm listening."

"Well, according to her, I was born in October, during Howl Week, an annual event where all the students crammed into a big cabin on Humboldt Bay and celebrated the anniversary of Ginsberg's first reading of his famous piece. Sylvia's midwife informed her that I was about to arrive any moment and she should stay in the city, but apparently, my mother's 'Celestial Advisor' told her not to worry. She told Sylvia that I would come when the stars were perfectly aligned and not a minute sooner."

I paused, took a sip of tea, and stole a quick glance at Chen. He sat quietly and still and appeared genuinely interested. So, I went on.

"Sylvia said she felt contractions early in the evening during the reading of a poem called 'An Exercise in Love,' but she ignored them. Her water broke during 'Smokey the Bear Sutra.' By the time some guy named Jack was in the middle of a piece from *On the Road*—the part about Ginsberg's horn, 'ta-tup-tater-rara...ta-tup-tade-rara...' the pain was so bad Sylvia crawled under a table and stretched out on the floor. She said it was the only bare surface available.

"Everyone was banging on pots and pans or bongo drums, and stomping, and laughing, and yelling, and splashing wine and beer, and passing joints. That's when one of the other women noticed her and swooped down with a pillow, ready to help with the delivery. When Jack got to the part where he was reading, 'Hey now baby-baby, make a way, make a way, it's Lampshade coming your way...' well, I came sliding out. And, I'm told, I screamed louder than all of them put together. Jack stopped reading—they all stopped everything and crowded around the table to cheer me on.

"Somebody asked Sylvia what she was going to call me. Because she couldn't remember the name she'd picked out, she looked up, through the table legs, past the sea of stoned hippies to a desk on the other side of the room. There was a bottle of ink on top of someone's manuscript. My mother read the label out loud. Sheaffer. Then she read the color, Blue. And, that's how I was named Sheaffer Blue. At least, that's how my mother tells the story."

Chen waited a moment, then asked about my father.

"She isn't sure—she thinks it was one of the guys named Neal. There were three Neals but only one with an Irish brogue, and given my hair..." I stopped and watched for Chen's reaction.

His eyes narrowed, he turned away slightly, looked like maybe he was doing a math problem in his head. Finally, he faced me. "October," he said, "when? The first part, or toward the end of the month?"

That threw me. I didn't see that coming at all. "Eighth. October eighth. Why?"

He seemed to concentrate for a moment before answering. "Well, that makes you a Libra. I wouldn't have guessed that. Scorpio. I would have guessed Scorpio for sure." He shook his head.

Wow. I would never, in a bazillion years, have guessed that this high-ranking detective, this seemingly conservative man, would know about astrology. Or, to have an opinion about my astrological sign. "Well," I said, "that 'Celestial Advisor' was wrong about my timing. I was a month premature. Sylvia always figured I arrived early because I didn't wanna miss the party."

Chen started to laugh. A big, unrestrained laugh. He laughed so hard he shook the bed. At that moment, I realized that I *really* liked hearing David Chen laugh.

# 23

Elaine hit the contact for her daughter. Beverly picked up on the first ring.

"What do you want?"

"There's something you need to know about your husband. It's not pretty. If it ever leaks out to the police, or worse, the press, it might ruin the lovely life you've arranged for yourself. And it would weaken the political clout I have in this town and—"

"Get to the point."

Elaine ignored the interruption. "There's already that detective called Chen or Chan, or something like that, snooping around, and he's got that small-time insurance investigator playing tag team. I don't think the offer we extended to her is going to work." Elaine paused a moment. She chose her next words carefully. "Look, I know we don't always see eye to eye. Nonetheless, in this case, we should help each other out. We need to come up with a plan to protect our investments."

She waited and listened to her daughter sigh, and then to the click of a lighter. She could almost smell the smoke as she heard Beverly take a drag.

"All right. I'll meet you at Anthony's in an hour. We can grab a table on the deck. There's nobody there this time of day, so we'll have privacy, and, at the same time, we'll be in a public place, in case we need to have...you know...witnesses. Bye."

Elaine stood for a moment and looked at the photo of her daughter in her phone contacts. Beverly was a strong, polished woman. Educated, poised, and wealthy. She had the world by a string. And yet, without even knowing what she was going to hear, or what kind of plans they might make, she was already looking ahead to an alibi. Elaine shook her head. How and when did her beautiful little girl become so much like her mother?

# 24

My nose crinkled with the smell of brewing coffee. I stayed still for a moment and breathed in that heavenly scent and something else, equally as appealing. Chen. His scent on the pillow. His scent on my skin. I eased my eyes open and focused on the soft, pale light filtering through panels of gauzy fabric pulled across the French doors. I listened. Other than a faint sound that must have come from the coffeemaker, the room was silent. Chen's black robe draped neatly over the back of a chair—a single sheet of notepaper lay face up on the table. I slipped out of bed and into the robe, tied the belt, and read Chen's note:

*Sheaffer—*
*Coffee will brew at eight. Fruit in the refrigerator, croissants in the microwave. Wish I could give you a ride home—but I'm booked all day. Cab fare in the kitchen. Stay as long as you like—the door will lock behind you.*

*P.S. You're lovely. Do you know that?*
                                            *David*

I swallowed, folded the note, stashed it in the pocket of his robe, and wandered into the front room. Golden rays splashed across the marble floors and glistened on the water in the fountain. I nodded to the fish and kept moving—straight to that coffee. Chen had tucked a fifty-dollar bill under a mug and, true to his words, two croissants nestled in a bakery bag in the microwave oven. The refrigerator held a bowl of bite-sized squares of pineapple, papaya, and mango covered with plastic wrap. I could tell everything was fresh, and I wondered if Chen had gone out, shopped, and prepped the food while I slept in his bed. The thought gave me a warm, squishy sort of feeling—one I would usually abhor. Somehow, today, I liked it.

I took an almond croissant and a cup of black coffee outside to the deck and looked over Seattle. The city appeared light, peaceful, and calm. Thoughts of Shirley's burned body, Chen's close call with a bullet, a smack to my head, and the attempted drowning all tried to burble up and ruin the moment. I pushed them away and breathed in the cool morning air. I decided that nothing could ruin this perfect day.

After a second cup, I washed the mug and the coffeepot, made the bed, and took a shower. I kept hoping that Chen would come home—even for a short break, one long enough to repeat... *Don't be ridiculous. His note was clear. He'll be busy all day. I should get busy, too.*

On the way through the marina parking lot, my friend with the new boyfriend waved to me. It was all I could do not to stop and tell her about my evening. About David's slow, warm touch. About the scent he left in the sheets. I felt a little stupid in a giddy sort of way, so I simply returned the wave and kept going.

"Morning, Sunshine!" One neighbor called out as I bounced past his boat.

"Musta had a gooooood night!" Another grinned and waved from his cockpit.

I laughed and waved back. Yes. A perfect night.

Three trips up the dock to load laundry in the marina's machines. A glance at my phone. No texts. I wondered if he'd like the poems of Langston Hughes. Four trips to the community trash bins with bursting garbage bags. No texts. I considered learning how to cook. Three buckets of hot soapy water, four buckets of rinse water, two new sponges, and a bag of fresh kitty litter later, I hauled myself up to the marina bathroom for my second shower of the day. Still, no texts. No calls. At least not the one I waited for. Oh well, I thought, no worries. He's busy.

*Aquarius... A quaaarie ous...* Lilly's ring tone blasted louder than the hair-dryer.

"Hey, Lil. What's up?"

"Oh, Blue, I'm so excited, you won't believe this, I got a job, and now I'm a part-time driver of the van for the *Evergreen Gardens Retirement Home*—you know, the one we went to—only on weekends and evenings and maybe on some days and today..." She paused and gulped a breath.

"Lil, slow down," I said. I knew it was a moot point.

"So, I'm going to give Charlie a ride to the marina to have lunch with his friends there and Ray would come and help me get the wheelchair down but he has to work and can't and I promised so I want to pick you up and the two of us and maybe that nice man Bud can..." Again, she sucked in a breath.

I laughed. "Yeah, sure. Of course, I'll help. Get on over here. I have to feed the cat and grab my bag. Come on down to the boat. See you soon."

Lilly stood at the bottom of the companionway and stared at *Ink Spot*'s salon. "Who *are* you and where did you hide my best friend? Maybe I'm on the wrong boat. Maybe I'm sleepwalking. If that's the case, I hope I didn't leave that poor old man alone in the van in the parking lot."

The cat brushed back and forth against my legs as I dumped a can of tuna into his bowl and broke it up with a fork. While the cat attacked the fish, I washed and dried the fork and slipped it into a drawer. Lilly gasped and faked a faint.

"Lighten up," I said. "I can clean my boat once every ten years if I want to."

"Oh my God!" Lilly slapped her forehead with the palm of her hand. "I get it. It *has* to be. You are in *love*!"

"Don't be ridiculous. Now, come on. Don't we have to give an old man and his wheelchair a ride down a dock?" I grinned and gave her arm a light punch.

Bud, Geraldine, and Dorothy waited for us at the head of Dock W. They had planned to lay a thick sheet of plywood over the steps so we could roll Charlie's chair down to the dock. However, unable to find the right ramp material, we went with Plan B. I slipped my arms under Charlie's, Lilly looped hers under his knees, the two other women stood on either side, and when we lifted him, they grabbed each other by the wrists under his bottom and made a sling. Then, bit by bit, we clumped down the stairs. Bud followed with the wheelchair. It was slow going, accompanied by a great deal of grunting and laughing and a significant amount of swearing. I guessed it wasn't the safest method of transporting a disabled person, but the four close friends obviously enjoyed every moment. I caught Lilly's eye. She smiled and winked. I began to understand why my friend had so much fun working with the elderly.

Once we settled Charlie back in his chair, Lilly led the way down the dock. She danced and twirled with her arms stretched wide. Bud, Geraldine, and Dorothy stumbled along behind, frequently bumping into each other. Each time it happened, they all giggled like preteens at an R-rated movie. "What's up with them?" I asked as I pushed Charlie's wheelchair toward Dorothy's houseboat.

"My guess is they found the last of Shirley's magic brownies," he said. He shook his head. "You'd think they'd grow out of that behavior. You'd think they'd act like adults." Then he twisted around and looked at me. "Can you hurry it up a little? There's a double Scotch waiting for me in that houseboat."

Once we got everyone safely aboard and settled around Dorothy's dining table with drinks and munchies, Lilly headed to the kitchen to work on their lunch. It occurred to me that the old friends had some catching up to do so I wandered away from the dining table into the living room and plopped down on the sofa with the intention of taking a short nap before we ate. I had closed my eyes and had prepared to float into memories of my evening with Chen when I felt a nudge on my arm.

"Here, dear." Geraldine stood in front of me, smiling. She held a round tin decorated with an old-fashioned Christmas scene. "We thought you might want to join the party. This is Shirley's last gift to us. Pick out a small one to start. They're stronger than you think." She handed the tin to me, covered her mouth with one hand, and giggled softly before she shuffled back to the dining table.

I glanced down and considered the situation. Pot brownies are always a favorite of mine—you get a sugar buzz and stoned, sort of a two-for-one high. However, when Chen called, I wanted to be straight, and ready. I fished my phone from my back pocket. No texts. No calls. I glanced at the tin. Oh well, maybe—perhaps—a small one.

Under the tight lid, one lone, rather large brownie sat on a sheet of waxed paper. I picked it up, lifted the sheet of paper, and counted twelve more chocolate squares tucked together on a second waxy sheet. I grinned. What a nice gift. Shirley's final gift to her friends. Marijuana brownies baked and hidden...I stopped. Hidden where? In plain sight?

I peeled the next layer of paper aside, left it and the brownie on the sofa, grabbed the tin, and hurried to the dining table where Bud sat spinning a long and compli-cated tale of adventure. Even though I knew it was rude, I couldn't wait for him to finish. "Sorry to butt in but I have to ask something. Where did you guys find these brownies?"

No one seemed to mind the interruption as they happily launched into their story of how they'd worked together to distract the young police officers guarding Shirley's houseboat.

"You see," Bud explained, "We all knew Shirley kept her brownies in her freezer—she'd been doing that for years."

"And we had to get them before the police found them," Dorothy added. "Because Shirley didn't need them for medical reasons...she, well we, like getting..." she giggled.

"High," Bud filled in.

"You should have seen Geraldine flopping around on the deck," Dorothy said.

"Yes, I was quite the actress," Geraldine beamed. She patted the empty chair beside her. "Come, join us."

I scooched a chair between the two women and sat the tin on the table. On a hunch, I carefully pulled out a brownie, and sat it on the edge of Dorothy's salad plate. Then I lifted the other gooey squares, one by one, until I reached a second sheet of waxed paper. I pulled it out. Beneath it lay a spread of aluminum foil, cut in a circle, wedged tight against the tin's rounded sides. Using my thumbnail, I eased the circle up enough to get an edge and gave a tug.

No one spoke as I gingerly pulled a thin, homemade wax paper packet out from under the sheet of foil. The wax paper was sealed with several pieces of tape. I didn't want to tear anything, so I took my time in easing past the tape. The four friends remained silent as they watched me work. Finally, I removed three envelopes from the packet.

The first contained the title and beneficiary pages of a life insurance policy. As I read the terms of the policy out loud, Dorothy wept quietly. Geraldine looped her arm around her friend. The men sat still—grim-faced.

The second envelope carried a brief, carefully constructed Last Will and Testament. I didn't look up while I read this, but I could feel the intensity of the emotions around that dining table.

Finally, I pulled a single sheet of yellow, lined paper from the third envelope. At that, Dorothy gasped, and Geraldine covered her face with her hands.

"Sweet Jesus," Bud blurted.

Charlie leaned forward in his wheelchair, his hand outstretched to me. "If you don't mind," he said, "I'd like to read that to the group."

Larry's letter to Shirley, written on the night of his twenty-first birthday, was printed by hand in tight, cramped letters. While he'd peppered the message with sappy phrases about true love and undying devotion— most of it expressed fear. Even though the death of the port commissioner was an accident, Larry had been terrified of getting caught, of ruining his life, and of spending the rest of his life in jail. He took all the blame for pushing and killing the commissioner. He even wailed on about hiding the body. He didn't mention Shirley's part in the event—didn't even put her at the scene. Larry had dated both the top and bottom and signed it with his full name.

The letter was a confession and the most incriminating evidence a prosecutor could ever wish for.

It occurred to me that Shirley had probably kept the letter for sentimental reasons, at least initially. It represented a final goodbye from the man she loved. Probably wasn't until much later when she learned about the life path Larry had followed, and about the family he'd married into, that she had seen the potential value of his farewell message. To her credit, it appeared that she hadn't tried to use the letter for personal gain. She'd only kept it around as a means of protecting her home and her friends. My admiration for Shirley soared.

After a sobering discussion, the group decided that at least for the time being, they would remain calm and quiet about their secret. Dorothy opened another bottle of wine and poured another double Scotch for Charlie. Lilly popped in from the kitchen, helped herself to half a brownie, and then went back to preparing lunch.

I was too wired to eat. The rational, responsible, grown-up me wanted to call Chen immediately—this was critical information, and he needed to know it ASAP. But the me who wanted to gush my emotions to my friend in the parking lot earlier, longed for him to call first. I'd be cool, sexy, tease a little, and then casually toss in, *oh, by the way, guess what I found*? Conflicted, muddled, and excited all at once, I decided the only answer was to clear my head with a late afternoon sail.

Bud begged to join me, saying that it had been years since he'd been on the water and that this might be his last chance. I wanted time alone. Still, the old sailor looked so sad, and so forlorn, that I relented. Lilly offered her car as she planned to spend the rest of the day with Dorothy, Geraldine, and Charlie. Before leaving Dock W, Bud insisted that I wait while he stopped at his houseboat to grab his lucky boating cap. The floppy-rimmed Tilley knock-off was frayed, dirty, and well-loved. I could tell it had weathered many days on the water.

Once on *Ink Spot*, I watched as the elderly fellow coiled lines, and I recognized that far-away, dream-filled look that sailors have when they stand on a rolling deck, face lifted to the sun, salty breeze in the hair. My discovery under the brownies had touched each of Shirley's friends—that was obvious. And, although I wasn't sure why, I suspected her words had touched Bud most deeply. He, too, needed this time at sea.

Maybe I was distracted because of my role in solving a decades-old mystery and finding the evidence that would most likely put Lawrence Winslow behind bars. Or, it could have been the mellow high from that small bite of Shirley's brownie that fogged my thinking. Possibly, I might have slipped up, because I was still glowing from the love and kindness that poured from the pages of Shirley's Last Will and Testament. And, well...there was the *odd* chance, that the scent and touch of Chen lingering in my thoughts made me dreamy and unfocused. Whatever the reason, I made a critical mistake. A mistake so serious that Neptune was sure to record it in his great log. I left the dock without checking *Ink Spot*'s fluids. If I had gone below to the engine room, I would have noticed the smell of gasoline as it trickled from a cut in the side of a plastic fuel can, and I would have found her, crouched in the shadows of the V-berth, waiting.

# 25

The wind seemed perfect for a sail around the bay, so we went through the locks, out through the channel, and into open water. Bud served as a competitent crew member. He handled the lines, followed the instructions of the U.S. Army Corps of Engineers, and remained alert and stable in his post at the bow. When we slid from the locks, he joined me in the cockpit as I maneuvered out of the channel and into Puget Sound. Shirley's cat sat in a pile of line next to the mast. We made a happy little crew.

"Mind if I poke around? Look at your gear?" He nodded toward starboard. "Been so long I can hardly remember what's what."

"Sure, have at it," I said. "We'll be in open water in a few minutes, and then I'm going to hand you the helm while I go forward and raise the main. Okay?"

He didn't have to answer—his kid-waiting-for-Santa expression said it all. I watched, amused, as he fished around in the miscellaneous gear I kept stashed in the space below the lazarette. He pulled out a tangled wad of lines, a couple of moldy PFDs and an orange plastic box.

"Oh wow," he said when he opened the box, "I forgot all about these. Charlie and I used to fire ours off on the fourth of July. Regular cowboys, we were." He chuckled as he cocked my flare gun.

"Well, Wyatt, be careful with that. I don't want you blowing a hole in my boat."

He offered a mock salute, set the plastic gun on the cockpit sole, and turned his attention to the jumble of lines. "I'm gonna straighten these out for you," he said. He closed the lazarette cover, sat down, and with furrowed brow, concentrated on unknotting the salt-hardened lump. I smiled as I watched him work. Nothing quite like a boat project to challenge the mind and keep a body young.

A few minutes past the final buoy I slowed the engine and pointed *Ink Spot's* bow into the wind. She'd started her slow, graceful turn when I heard a sharp "click." I jerked my head toward the companionway and found myself staring down the barrel of a shiny, chrome-plated pistol. Beverly Winslow braced on the companionway hatch and steadied herself against the gentle roll of the deck. Dressed in khaki pants, a striped long-sleeved tee, and canvas deck shoes, she looked like any other urban sailor, that is, except for the tight, black leather gloves. She held the pistol firm and steady, and she pointed it directly at me. I felt my hands go clammy on the wheel.

Although Bud must have missed the sound, he caught my expression and followed my gaze. His jaw dropped and he stood. "What the..."

Beverly's eyes flicked toward starboard. "Sit down, Grandpa." She growled her words like a low warning from a large cat—no hint of nervousness or fear.

Bud started to sit, and then, in a flash of his earlier cowboy spirit, he lifted the heavy knotted lines and flung them at Beverly.

She was fast and easily avoided the projectile. With a single, quick move, she stepped forward and backhanded the pistol against Bud's head. Blood splattered, and he stumbled toward the helm. She moved in and hit him a second time. He crumpled to the cockpit sole.

"Bud!" I bent to grab him.

"Leave him," Beverly said. "He's not your problem. I am." Again, she pointed the gun at my chest. Her eyes were narrow and cold, her gaze unflinching. "Remember me, Miss Pretend Investigator?"

I straightened and nodded. My throat was so dry I could barely speak. Despite the warmth of the late afternoon, I shivered. "You're Beverly Winslow. I croaked out the words. "Larry's wife."

She gave a short, harsh laugh. "Right. Wife of the very wealthy and very lame-brained Port Commissioner Lawrence Winslow."

Bud groaned, and I bent toward him.

"I said, leave him!" Beverly stepped closer to me. "There isn't anything you can do to help him. Or yourself. Put your hands on that wheel and stay still."

I tried to swallow as I grasped the helm. "What do you want?" My voice sounded strangled and faint, and I wondered if I'd actually spoken out loud.

"I want my life back. My life before this whole dock project started. Before I'd ever heard of that old hag, Shirley."

My mind raced, but my body felt heavy—weighted down. "I...I don't understand. What do you care about your mother's project? And why are you here, on my boat? And...why the gun?"

Beverly took a small step back, stood with her legs slightly apart and braced against the side of the companionway. She raised the gun a fraction. "Before that damned dock project, I had everything I wanted. Big house, money, easily manipulated husband. My life was perfect. Until she...that Shirley person...butted in. I knew Larry was rekindling an old relationship with her, the signs were everywhere. The way he looked at that picture of the two of them, the hushed phone calls."

"Did *you* burn down the houseboat?" I asked.

Beverly shook her head. "No. I had nothing to do with that. I only went to see her, to make sure I knew what was going on before I confronted my husband. I could have taken care of everything by dealing with him. Then I saw his jacket on her sofa. That's when I lost it. I certainly wasn't going to give up everything to some withered old hippy woman."

"But, but..." The only thing I could think of was to keep Beverly talking. We weren't that far out of the channel, so the chance of another boat cruising by was good. I hoped that anyone sliding past would see Beverly holding a gun on me and would radio for help. It was my only hope. "Shirley...she was killed in that fire."

Beverly narrowed her eyes. "No. That old bird was dead and gone before that fire ever started. When I saw his jacket, I got so angry that I was going to call Larry and read him the riot act, right there, right in front of her. But when I opened my handbag for my phone, I saw my EpiPen. I didn't even think. I grabbed it and jabbed it right into that scrawny neck of hers." Another cold laugh. "She flailed around a minute or so, then jerked backward, and then, bye-bye Shirley. My guess? Heart attack. I didn't care. She was gone, that's all that mattered. I dragged her into the bedroom, grabbed Larry's jacket and left. The fire was a lucky stroke. No fingerprints, nothing. I would have been in the clear. Except for that nosey detective. That asshole should have taken the hint when mother shot at him. Too bad she can't aim for shit."

I gasped. Chen! Where was he now? I glanced around, looked for another boat—we were alone. *Keep her talking, Blue. Keep her talking.*

"But Beverly, there wasn't any evidence of foul play. The fire covered up everything. No one would ever have known." I said.

Beverly nodded. "Yes, that's what I thought, too. But that detective keeps digging. He won't leave things alone. I'm afraid that he might find out about my husband's dirty old secret and I can't have that." She shrugged. "But that poor Mr. Detective, he's going to have a little accident in his rental car. Sad—it's such a nice vehicle. Sad for him, too, I guess. And since you were working with him, well, too bad for you, as well."

"Chen?" A jolt of current hit my chest and my throat squeezed shut. I felt dizzy, and, for a moment, I almost forgot about the gun aimed at my heart.

"Oh, I see." Beverly raised an eyebrow and smiled with tight, pursed lips. "You have a thing for that nosey detective. Well, don't worry, he'll join you soon enough."

Her comment slapped me back. "You...you can't kill us." I stuttered. "Everyone knows my boat and my dinghy. They'll notice the sails flapping or, someone will..."

Beverly cut me off. "Shut up. One shot and you're gone. Another one makes sure gramps here is gone, too. I've been watching you, and I've learned your patterns. No one will come looking for you. Nobody cares. Once I'm halfway back to shore, you and gramps, and your crappy old boat, will disappear, and my life can get back on track."

My tongue felt thick and my chest was so tight I could barely breathe. "What do you mean, my boat will disappear?"

Beverly held the gun steady with one hand and with the other she reached into her pants pocket. She pulled out a small box about the size of a deck of cards. "Your boat is full of gas fumes. When I press the digital code, this little baby will throw a remote switch on a clicker sitting on your table. Only takes one spark. Works on boats, rental cars, anything." She slipped the device back into her pocket. "It's amazing what you can buy online these days." With that, she jerked her head toward the davit on the stern. "Now, lower the dinghy and don't try anything. If I have to shoot you before you get it in the water, no big deal. A little more work for me—that's all." She gestured with the gun. "Hurry up."

I swallowed hard and slowly turned toward the stern. As I reached for the line that supported the dinghy, I noticed Bud from the corner of my eye. He had come to and had somehow managed to grasp the flare gun without Beverly or me noticing. To give him a distraction I looked over my shoulder at Beverly. She stood in front of the companionway—both hands on the pistol.

"This always sticks," I said. I looked up toward the davit's pulley.

Beverly focused on me—she followed my gaze. She didn't notice Bud as he pulled the trigger of the flare gun. I spun around in time to see a blaze of light strike Beverly's arm, bounce off, and fly down through the open companionway to the salon below.

# 26

## The New Moon

I felt it before I heard it. A soft, low, distant hum cocooned me. I floated in a cloud of the steady drone. I think I sighed. And then, things changed. The rhythmic drone moved up an octave and shattered into stretches of a harsh buzz punctuated by bits of silence. The cloud became riddled with sharp, irritating, pebble-like objects that pressed against my skin. I tried to roll over, to adjust to a more comfortable position. The vibration went higher, and closer, and turned staccato.

"Thank you for coming. Namaste."

The sound was familiar. Language. I recognized the reverberation even though I couldn't understand the terms. A moment later the words made sense, and an excruciating pain gripped my entire body. I think I groaned.

"Nurse! Call the nurse. She's awake!"

Lilly's voice. The pain increased. I opened my eyes. At first, I saw only fuzzy shadows—grays and muted whites. Slowly, objects and faces came into focus.

"Blessed be!" Lilly leaned close. I could tell that her cheeks were wet with tears. "You're awake, Blue. Baby Blue. Welcome back, dear one."

A woman dressed in pale green scrubs nudged her aside and touched my wrist. In my peripheral vision, I saw a tangle of tubes, and bottles, and a forest of flowers. In one corner of the room, a bouquet of helium balloons floated and bobbed at the end of bright ribbons tied to a chair.

"Lil?"

"I'm right here, honey." She stood next to the woman in green by the side of what I now realized was a hospital bed. Lilly sobbed and rocked back and forth from one foot to the other. The women in scrubs fiddled with the tubes and the instruments and watched digital numbers on a screen. She looked at Lilly.

"She's stable. You can invite her friends in for a few minutes but make it short. I'm pretty sure she'll need more pain meds soon. And she needs to rest."

Lilly, two senior women, an elderly man in a wheelchair, and a female cop crowded together next to the bed. Except for Lilly I didn't know them, couldn't remember their names. Still, I felt their energy—friendly and safe. The man leaned forward from his chair and gently placed one hand on my foot. He pulled it back the moment I yelped.

"Oh, I'm so sorry. Does your foot hurt?"

"Everything hurts." I managed a thin smile and tried to joke. "Where the hell is that Mack truck? Did anybody get the license number?" Nobody laughed. I tried it again. "Okay, fess up. Which one of you practiced your kickboxing moves on me?" Still, they didn't seem to get my attempts at humor. I tried a different tack. "Okay, then, who *are* you? And what happened to me?"

One by one they introduced themselves—Dorothy, Geraldine, and Charlie. The young police officer smiled but didn't speak. No one answered my second question.

"Well? Damn it! What happened to me?" Every word, every breath, caused pain. I felt like I'd been beaten, or maybe like I'd fallen from the roof of a two-story house, or had jumped from a bridge and hit the water hard. Finally, one of the seniors, the woman who had introduced herself as Dorothy, cleared her throat and spoke.

"You were in a boating accident, honey. A serious boating accident."

I closed my eyes and attempted to breathe without pain. It wasn't possible, so I forced myself to concentrate on what she'd said. A boating accident. What boat? What accident? I couldn't organize my thoughts, and my brain seemed to pound against my skull. I opened my eyes and looked at the people gathered close to me—their faces strained with worry, fear, and something else. Try as I might, I couldn't read their emotions. I could barely stay focused.

"Tell me what happened." My words came out in a slurred croak. The fellow in the wheelchair, Charlie, nodded and swallowed. He glanced at the others and lifted two fingers. Dorothy nodded back to him, then she reached out and took Geraldine's hand.

Charlie cleared his throat. "You and Bud went for a sail. There was an explosion," he said. He paused, "can you remember anything?"

Once more, I closed my eyes. I remembered the wind. Cool and clean. And I heard an old man's laughter. Bud. Yes. I *did* remember him. I saw his grin and the ridiculous cap he wore. Then I thought I heard another sound. Through the beeping of the instruments next to the hospital bed, through someone's nervous cough, I thought I heard a yowl. A cat. I remembered the cat! My eyes snapped open. "What happened to the cat?"

Lilly answered. "They found you clinging to a chunk of wood—a door or something—and that cat was perched on your back yowling to high heaven. Don't worry about him. He's fine, and he's eating enough for an entire family of cats." Her comment seemed to break the tension, and they all laughed—a little.

"You better give that critter a name," Charlie said. "After living through a fire and an explosion, looks like he's gonna be around for a long time."

I forced a smile. My jaw ached. "Any ideas?"

"Well," he scratched his head. "The name Lucky comes to mind."

More soft chuckles from the group. I counted them. Something was missing. *Someone* was missing. Oh yes. Bud. The old man with the silly cap. He was missing. "And Bud?"

Charlie looked down at his lap. Lilly made a gulping sound. Dorothy let go of Geraldine's hand and placed her palm against my cheek. Her skin felt cool and soft. "He didn't make it, dear," she said.

I wanted to ask more, to make sense of what seemed completely senseless, but my thoughts were jumbled, and my nerves were on fire. I couldn't think through the pain. The next thing I remember was the nurse fiddling with the tubes. A warm wave of relief washed over me.

The next day—at least I assumed it was the next day—a good-looking man in a black leather jacket paid a visit. He walked with a slight limp and held his left arm bent and pressed close to his side. His right arm wrapped around a vase filled with an enormous bouquet of white and yellow roses. A small envelope hung from a tangle of pale green curling ribbon. He pushed a hospital-issued water pitcher aside and placed the vase on the nightstand next to my bed. As he bent down, I caught a whiff of his cologne. Nice, I thought. Too short for me and probably uptight but still...it was clear this man knew me and cared about me. Lines of concern etched his face, despite his overt attempt to appear calm and cheerful. While, except for Lilly, I couldn't remember anyone's name—even minutes after they'd introduced themselves—I could tell when a person was important to me. And in some strange way, I knew this man played a special role in my life—an incredibly special role. Weird, I know.

"Sheaffer." He pulled a chair next to the bed and sat down. "I was in California when Lilly texted me. Willow had a part in a play—I got the text in the middle of the performance. But I grabbed the next flight out. I came as soon as I could."

He glanced down and grimaced at the sight of my right hand where my skin puffed up black and blue under the strips of tape holding IV needles in place. Then he touched my shoulder ever so gently, ever so briefly.

I had no idea who he was, or who Willow was, or why they were in California. A play? Maybe Willow was an actress. I strained to think but the effort caused shooting pains in my head, so I decided to simply go along—to just pretend I knew him and his Willow.

"How did she do?" I asked. "In the play?"

"Oh, cute. You know. Kids."

He went on for a while about this child, her school activities, how he'd told her all about me and how brave I was and how much she looked forward to meeting me. I gathered this Willow child was his daughter or at least a favored niece. I tried to nod and smile and look interested but the whole thing was a lot of work, and I grew sleepy. He obviously noticed, because he switched subjects.

"So, Sheaffer, Lilly tells me you're having some memory issues. But," he leaned in a bit closer—close enough for a nice second hit of that cologne. "This is important. We are very close to figuring out who killed Shirley, but we, um...I, need your help. Who was on your boat? What happened? Can you remember anything? Even something small might help."

I shook my head. "I'm so sorry," I whispered.

A thought, maybe an emotion, or an understanding flickered across his face.

"You don't know who I am, do you?"

I could see a sadness registered in his eyes. I wanted to reassure him, and I wanted to know him—I honestly did. But I had only questions. Was he my brother? A cherished friend? Could we be lovers? Fortunately, the shift nurse rescued both of us as she hustled into the room with a tray of medicines and supplies.

"I'm sorry sir, but visiting hours are over. We need to change her meds, and she's probably getting tired." She glanced over at me. "Are we tired?"

The man sighed, stood, pushed the chair against the wall where he'd found it, and paused to look at me.

"Don't worry," he said. "I'm here for you, and everything is going to be okay."

His words sounded somehow familiar and reassuring. I offered a weak but sincere smile.

Before he'd made it to the door, the nurse had dismissed him and was busy fiddling with the tangle of tubes leashing me to bottles and bags of clear liquids.

"Here now." She pushed the plunger on a syringe emptying into one of the tubes. "This will help you sleep. Okay now, anything else before I go?"

"Yes." I motioned toward the nightstand. "Could you hand me the card on those roses?"

She removed the card from the small envelope, handed it to me without a glance, and spun out of the room with her tray of soon-to-be-discarded supplies.

A sunset-orange light slipped between the slats of the hospital room's blind and fringed the edge of my bed. Just enough light to read the handwritten message on the card.

*Sheaffer –*
*I've got you. You're safe.*
            *David*

# 27

Over the next few days, my brain began to clear. At times, I wished it wouldn't. Lilly slowly helped me reconstruct the hours before my sail with Bud, and then she gently tried to ease me into remembering what had happened on the boat. I worked hard to focus on clearing the fog that clouded my thoughts. There were definitely gaps—big gaps, and I couldn't seem to close them. Whenever Lilly visited, the young policewoman accompanied her. As I struggled to recall my experiences, the officer wrote in a thin, spiral-bound notebook. I wanted to give her the information she needed but more than that, I wanted to know—really know—what had happened to me and to well...everything. One day, Lilly stopped our conversation and asked me if I was okay, if was this too hard for me, was it too painful to continue?

"You're being very brave," she said. "I'd be a blubbery mess if I went through all the stuff you went through. I don't think I could even go a full five minutes without breaking into tears."

"I'm okay," I said. "Really, I'm okay."

Lilly took me at my word, although I noticed a deep frown cross the officer's face. The truth was, I suspected, I wasn't okay. I suspected that something wasn't quite right. After all, from what I'd been told, I'd been in a major accident in which a kind, elderly man had been killed, I'd narrowly escaped death, and my boat—my only home—had been blown to smithereens. But even when Lilly prompted me, or I looked at the photos the policewoman presented, I had no emotional response. No tears, no fear, no sorrow. Nothing. I wasn't even angry and that was the worst of it. I didn't feel like swearing or throwing something across the room. I didn't even have a reaction the day David Chen gave me a folded note. A love note of sorts.

He would stop by every evening after Lilly and the others had gone home. Most of the time he sat by my bed and asked questions—lots and lots of questions. He'd repeat those questions over and over again, and he kept circling back, almost as if he were trying to catch me in a lie, but I knew that wasn't the case. I could tell he was frustrated with himself. He knew he was close to figuring out a puzzle, but close wasn't good enough. I'm sure he felt that I had the final pieces. I hoped I did and I hoped that I would be able to give them to him. But those pieces, along with a mental shoebox full of memories, were well-hidden behind a wall of throbbing, and often searing, headaches.

Sometimes, he simply talked to me as if we were longtime friends. He'd tell me about his daughter and her friends, about the house he was building in the burbs outside of San Francisco, and about his wife, who'd passed after a long struggle with cancer.

And sometimes, just to mix things up, I'd ask him a question.

"So, how'd you get the limp?"

"Oh, the limp," he'd said. "Not one of my finest moments."

I waited.

"You might not remember, but I told about you about my parents—both veterinarians. I probably mentioned how our house was always crawling with animals in various stages of health and recovery."

I didn't remember anything about his past, his parents, or the household full of critters but I smiled and nodded encouragement because I liked hearing his stories. I liked hearing his voice.

"Well, one of my jobs was to climb the tree in our backyard and rescue kittens when they got stuck up there. Not sure why, but every kitten we had seemed to get stuck in that old willow tree. I didn't mind going up—that was easy. But coming back down, holding a squirming baby cat—that was a pain. So, I got creative."

I smiled.

He sighed. "Well, I figured if I just grabbed onto one of those long, swaying branches, I could swing down—Tarzan-like—King of the Kitten Rescues. But, turns out those branches aren't as flexible or as strong as they look. With a tabby under one arm, I grabbed a branch and took a leap. You can probably guess the rest."

"And the kitten?"

"Not a scratch. But I was stuck in the house for a couple of weeks—which wasn't a big deal since I had the broken leg..."

These were my favorite visits as they helped me form a picture of this man, who seemed like a stranger but who felt so familiar.

On a few occasions, he'd flirt with me—light, gentle flirting. The evening he brought the note was one of those times. Although I think, for him, it may have been more serious than merely a playful tease.

"Hey Blue." He walked into the room with a vase filled with daisies and stalks of something purple. After finding a place for the flowers, he pulled a chair next to the bed and, after a few minutes of light chitchat about his day and my recovery process, he pulled a piece of paper from his jacket pocket and handed it to me.

"I'm trusting this will bring back some pleasant memories for you." He leaned forward—looked hopeful.

The paper was folded four times, and because my hand was still tethered to the IV, he helped me smooth it flat.

*Sheaffer—*
*Coffee will brew at eight. Fruit in the refrigerator, croissants in the microwave. Wish I could give you a ride home—but I'm booked all day. Cab fare in the kitchen. Stay as long as you like—the door will lock behind you.*

*P.S. You're lovely. Do you know that?*
*David*

I could feel him watching me as I read the words. I wanted to remember—obviously, this was important—obviously a note written on a morning following a night I *should* have remembered. But I didn't. And he knew it. The formal training he'd received to become a police detective wasn't required for him to read my face and to realize that the emotions he so much yearned for me to recall simply were not there.

He didn't stay much longer that evening—said he had to attend to a report for work. I imagined that he had to attend to a wounded heart.

When he'd left, I tucked the paper into the pages of a novel on the nightstand. I knew his message should have evoked feelings, but I felt nothing. I had utterly flatlined in the emotion department.

The doctor had told me my lack of emotions and my inability to cry was a normal reaction to brain injury, and she said that as I became less dependent on the pain meds, and as my body healed, my emotions would return. She was a no-nonsense, middle-aged woman who wore her hair in a tight chignon and a strand of pearls under her stethoscope. She stopped in every morning to check my chart, ask me a few questions, and to reduce the amount of medication prescribed to me.

One morning she left a business card on the table by my bed. "This is my friend's card," she said. "She's a trauma counselor—a good one. When you get out of here, you might want to give her a call."

I didn't think I needed a shrink. Mostly, I thought I needed to find a new job as Lilly told me my old gig was gone. She said something about the agency not having any clients—something about my old boss getting a janitorial position at the business school. But, other than that, she didn't elaborate. I didn't care.

But I did care that in addition to needing a new job, I needed a place to live. I tried to stay focused on the practical stuff.

Lilly obviously had a better grasp of the long term, because when she stopped by later that day and saw the card, she tucked it into her purse for safekeeping.

# 28

Following three evenings without a visit from David Chen, I assumed he'd given up on me. I figured he'd probably reasoned that I wasn't going to have answers to help him with his police work and that I was too broken to mend the relationship we, apparently, had once shared. But when I mentioned this to Lilly, she disagreed.

"No." She shook her head. Tiny bits of silver glitter fell from her dreadlocks and scattered over my bed. "Don't you remember? He stopped by two days ago— right about lunch time. He told us he was flying down to San Francisco to pick up his daughter. He's going to bring her up here for her birthday. He's got a big surprise for her and..." Lilly scrunched her face in concentration. "He's bringing her by the hospital to meet you. Today!" She looked at me and beamed.

You don't have many personal choices when you're stuck in a hospital bed, but I managed to convince Lilly to help me fix my hair and to locate a decent hospital gown with a thin matching robe. She cranked the bed to a seated position and propped me up on a pile of pillows. I'd just finished applying a layer of her pink lipstick when I heard the high-pitched voice of a little girl just outside the door.

"Do you think she'll like it, Daddy? I mean—do you think she likes unicorns?"

Chen laughed and for a split second I thought I had a flash of memory—something about that laugh—but it faded when he spoke. "Of course, honey. Who doesn't like unicorns?"

Unicorns indeed. Willow Chen skipped into my hospital room holding tight to a bright purple ribbon attached to a helium-filled Mylar balloon in the shape of a multicolored, grinning unicorn head. The thing had to be three feet in diameter and barely fit through the door. I wondered how that skinny little girl in her pink capris, black patent shoes, and glittery unicorn T-shirt wasn't pulled skyward by the huge balloon.

The second Willow saw me, she raced to the bed and, much to my complete surprise, released her grip on the ribbon and threw her arms around me.

"Sheaffer! I'm *soooo* happy to meet you!"

Lilly leaped up and chased after the disembodied, mythical creature floating slowly toward the ceiling. David Chen stood grinning at the foot of the bed and shrugged with a "what can you do?" gesture.

Willow packed the next thirty minutes with noisy, silly chatter about unicorns, school projects, something about a new puppy, and an invitation to come to San Francisco and see their new house.

"I have my own room!" Willow blurted out. "Guess what color?"

"Pink?" I took a stab at it.

"And purple, too." Willow nodded before twirling twice and skipping across the room to help Lilly tie the balloon ribbon to the back of a chair.

The whole thing was cute and fun but I grew tired, and my head pounded from the high-pitched laughter and the excitement. Chen noticed my discomfort and in the kindest, most loving way, ushered his daughter from the room.

"Walk her to the first floor?" he asked Lilly. She nodded and joined Willow in a skipping race down the hospital corridor.

Chen turned to me. "We're off to get a puppy," he said. I raised my eyebrows, and he rolled his eyes. Then he mouthed the words, "wish me luck."

The next thing that happened left me completely bewildered. I put it on my mental list of things I would have to manage, experiences I would have to sort out, and feelings I would have to untangle. Of course, I wasn't ready at that moment, but like so many other emotional events queued up for processing, this one got in line.

He smiled and took my right hand in both of his. His hands were warm and comforting and at that moment, I felt safe and secure.

"What Willow said about you coming to see the new house," he said. "She meant it. So do I. You're going to get out of here soon. I'm going to wrap up this case soon. And it's going to be my last case. I'm moving on."

I started to speak, but he interrupted.

"I'm quitting the department. Going to teach at the academy. They've offered me a good position, and I'm taking it. Willow needs more than a part-time father who works a dangerous job and is away most of the time. She needs a home, and family, and stability."

"And a puppy," I interjected.

He grinned and continued. "What I'm trying to say is that...well...you can be a part of that family." He gave my hand a light squeeze. "Think about it, okay?"

Without waiting for me to answer he released my hand, turned, and walked to the door.

# 29

Although my memory remained weak, my physical strength began to return. With the help of a hospital volunteer and daily visits from a physical therapist, I began taking short walks up and down the halls. I started taking showers without assistance and stayed awake longer than I slept. Dorothy, Geraldine, Charlie, and Lilly visited me every day and, while I suspected that it must have been a real trial for them to get around, I didn't question the visits. Another item I didn't question was the cost of the hospital and the medical treatment.

"One step at a time," the physical therapist had said during the only session when I'd tried to broach the subject. "Right now, your job is to get strong enough to check out of this place. After that, you can deal with the other stuff." I took him at his word.

I knew I was ready to leave the hospital and get on with my life the morning I woke, combed my hair, asked for a fresh hospital gown, and flirted with the young intern who followed the doctor on her rounds. When the doctor noticed the young man blushing from my slightly off-color comments, she declared that I'd be released the following morning.

"You're ready to go home," she said with an uncharacteristic grin.

It occurred to me that I didn't know where home was, so when Lilly and the police officer arrived for their daily visit, I shared both the good news about my release and my concerns with them. Lilly was thrilled and assured me that I had nothing to worry about as she and the others had worked out a plan. The policewoman congratulated me on such a rapid recovery and mentioned that she still had some unresolved questions, and that she'd like me to come down to the station to chat further once I'd gotten settled. I watched her place her notebook on the bedside table and join Lilly in collecting the cards, flowers, and balloons that festooned my room. Laughing and joking together, the two of them carried all of my worldly possessions away. As I watched the last of the balloons float out of my room, I made a vow to myself that not only would I find out exactly what had happened to me, but that somehow, I'd get my emotions back. And then, armed with what I knew would be grief and anger, I would seek revenge.

That evening, after dinner and visiting hours, I asked the night nurse if I could have a sleeping pill, as I was both excited and apprehensive about leaving in the morning. I didn't think I'd be able to sleep on my own and I wanted to start my new adventure strong and rested. She agreed. Within the hour, I slipped into a drowsy state, secure that soon my thoughts would drift away entirely and the dreamless hours that came with the sleep medication would begin. I welcomed the rest.

# 30

Lawrence Winslow motioned toward a leather chair next to the window in his home office. His once polished and professional expression had crumpled into a landscape of deep lines and dark under-eye bags. Elaine Dupont ignored him and stood—rigid—next to his desk. Years of expensive treatments kept her facial expressions neutral, but hurt and anger darted from her eyes. Lawrence sighed and walked across the room to stand facing her.

"What are we going to do? You know this is going to get out. They are going to find DNA or something that ties her to that explosion and to the death of that old geezer. This is going to ruin me."

"Ruin you?" Elaine came just shy of screeching her words. "You're worried about your career? You pathetic little weasel. Your wife is dead. My daughter is dead. And you're worried about your political career?"

Lawrence shrunk back—retreated—and sank into the leather chair he'd meant for her. He dropped his head and for just a moment, allowed grief to shake him. He could feel his mother-in-law watching him. He was pretty sure that he both disappointed and disgusted her. He took a deep breath and sat up straight.

"Okay, we've both suffered a great loss. And we'll never recover. But..." He held his hands out, palms up. "We have to be practical right now. Our lame story of her off on a shopping trip to Europe isn't fooling anyone. If—no—*when* that detective puts two and two together we are both going to prison for the rest of our lives. No matter how much money you throw at this, the game is up unless we get a new plan." He paused and watched her. He knew that she knew he was right—at least about this. Guessing he had the upperhand, he pressed on. "And, as I see it, this whole thing is your fault because of your ridiculous dock renovation project."

Elaine crossed the room in three steps and slapped Commissioner Lawrence Winslow across his face.

"You want to blame someone? You can blame your-self, you ignorant twit. You have never been able to think clearly. Who writes a murder confession as a Dear Jane note?" She pointed one long, sharp, manicured fin-ger directly at him. "This is *all* on you." She turned and walked back across the room, leaned against the edge of his polished walnut desk, and folded her arms across her chest.

They both stewed in silence for a few minutes until Lawrence finally caved. "Well, what are we going to do? Just let the cops arrest us? Skip the country?"

Elaine narrowed her eyes and pursed her lips into a thin, hard line. When she finally spoke, her words dropped like cubed ice into a crystal glass.

"The Seattle Police are not a problem. Most of them are stupid and the rest of them owe me. There are only two players we need to worry about. I'll deal with that detective—finish off what my daughter started. I know where she got the explosives—no worries there. You, idiot, are in charge of dealing with the girl. I don't care what you do or how you do it—just get rid of her." Elaine pushed away from the desk and walked to the office door. She paused with one hand on the knob.

"This is your last chance, Lawrence. Don't screw it up."

He listened to his mother-in-law's heels click against the marble of his hallway. He waited until he was sure she had left the house and then, Seattle Port Commissioner Lawrence Winslow, lowered his head to his hands and wept.

# 31

I'm not sure how long I'd been drifting toward sleep when I heard the words. The voice was low, deep, and male.

"I wanted to see you in bed," he said. "But this isn't exactly what I'd pictured." He whispered the words in my ear—so close I could feel his breath on my neck. He jabbed my shoulder with two fingers. "Well, too bad, because now, we need to have a little visit. I know you're not sleeping. Talk to me." He poked at me again.

I opened my eyes.

"Ah, that's better, Miss Blue." He pulled back and stood up straight. A thin line of light crept from under the door and lit his features—dark circles under his eyes betrayed worry and stress. That same light glinted off a small, compact pistol tucked into his waistband.

"Larry?" Despite the sleeping pill, I felt a surge of fear. Not only did I recognize this man, I realized that I was afraid of him. And, I realized that this fear was my first real feeling, other than pain, that I'd experienced since I'd arrived at the hospital. Somehow, it gave me strength—strength I decided, at that moment, to hide. "Larry?" I repeated the word in a feeble, weak-sounding voice.

"Yes, of course, it's me. You had to know that I would come. I have to know what she told you." His words were cold and flat.

"What? I don't understand. What do mean?"

"Of course, you understand." He leaned in close. "What did she say? What did my wife tell you? And why was she out sailing with you?"

I looked up at the clock opposite my bed. Someone should be making rounds soon. He saw my glance and let out a sharp, mean laugh.

"Oh, I'd forget that if I were you," he said. "I took care to create a distraction at the other end of the wing before I came to chat with you. A small fire in a recycling bin— just enough to keep the staff busy. Now..." His tone hardened. "It's time for you to tell me why my lovely bride— the woman who hated boats, hated going out on the water, even on a mega yacht—would be persuaded to join you for a sail on that rat trap you called home."

The human brain is a strange and mysterious wonder. In that worst—that shittiest—of all possible moments, my memory came flooding back. I instantly recalled the details of my last few minutes aboard *Ink Spot*. The entire scene raced by like a movie played on fast forward. I remembered every word Beverly Winslow had said. I remembered her voice, the hardness of her face, and the harshness of her laugh as she watched Bud stagger and slump to the cockpit sole. I gasped as I remembered how she'd gloated when she told me how she planned to kill Chen by blowing him up in his rental car the same way she intended to blow up my boat—with Bud and me aboard. These, I realized, were the memories Chen and the policewoman had been waiting for.

"Larry," I said, "I don't know what you're talking about. I don't remember anything."

"Yes, you do." He grabbed my left hand on the bruise where the IV had been and squeezed. "I'm not going to jail for something I didn't do. And I'm not going to jail for something that was an accident fifty years ago." He tightened his grip on my hand and twisted my skin.

The pain slashed my nerves. I gasped and pushed my words through gritted teeth.

"Let go, and I'll tell you what I remember."

He dropped my hand. "That's better. Be a good girl and tell me everything."

I willed myself to avoid looking toward the door. Even with a distraction, someone had to come by soon. I looked up at his face and realized he wasn't only mean and angry, Lawrence Winslow was scared. Not only was he frightened he'd be found guilty of the death of the port commissioner—a crime committed decades ago, he was afraid he'd be held responsible for Shirley's death as well. I tried to stall for time. I wanted to find out whatever I could from him, and so I played dumb.

"None of it made sense to me. She told me something about finding your jacket in the houseboat, and she was sure you and that old woman were having an affair."

He laughed. "Bev? Jealous of Shirley? That's a joke." Lawrence paused, looked at the floor, and seemed to be working through the information. "So, she was at the houseboat with Shirley. I wonder..."

"Look," I said, "I don't think you could kill anyone. I think that woman died in the fire. That's all. I'll put that in my report. I'll say that in court."

He snapped his attention back to me. "You're not going to court. You're not going to write any reports." He sneered at me. "In fact, you're not going to say anything to anyone. You're on your way to join my lovely wife—wherever she's gone."

He leaned in so close I could smell his breath, sour with fear. I wondered if my own breath matched that stink.

"But Lawrence, if you didn't do anything, you're free. What are you worried about?" Once more, I forced myself to look at him—not at the door. If I'd been a religious person, I would have been praying. As it was, I could only try to will the night nurse to make her rounds. *Come on, come on.*

"I thought you were smarter than that," he said. "I'm pretty sure you know I started that fire. I didn't kill Shirley. That much is true. I went to see her to try to talk her into giving me that letter. Thought I could charm her, but all that she wanted was to keep that crappy old dock for her and her cronies. She was a hoarder—kept everything. I knew she still had that letter."

"What letter?" I played innocent, tried to stall for time.

He looked past me, stared at the blank wall, and mumbled. "I didn't mean to hurt him. It was an accident. An accident on my twenty-first birthday. I killed Elaine's father. I was showing off for her, for Shirley—being a big man. I just pushed him, but the ground was muddy, and he slipped and fell back and hit his head on the corner of the bridge column. It was an accident."

Lawrence seemed far, far away. I stayed still—barely breathed—and let him talk.

"I was so freaked out. I was crying—some big man. Shirley had to take charge. We lifted him up and pushed him into the foundation frame. Then we covered him with dirt and leaves and rocks from the beach. When we were done, he was invisible. We were both exhausted and covered in mud, but we felt a little bit better. We both knew it was an accident—not our fault. And we thought it would—he would—just go away. We thought the construction guys would pour the cement in the morning and he'd be gone forever. And he was. Until that damned bridge repair."

Larry exhaled, became still, seemed to have drifted away, but before I could ask him more about the letter, he continued.

"It would have been fine even after they identified the bones. Nothing to connect us to the murder except that fucking letter. I was such an ass. I stayed up all night writing that letter to her—spelled out everything except for her part in things. I took every bit of the blame. Such a sap. I mailed it on my way out of town." He stopped and turned to me. "So, you understand, right?"

He held out his hands, palms up, like he was pleading with me, but I don't think he saw me. He was too far away. I didn't say a word. He let his hands drop, refocused on the wall, and continued. "When she wouldn't give me the letter, I left. I was so angry that I forgot my jacket. I went back that night to retrieve it and to try, one more time, to change Shirley's mind. I even took a bottle of good brandy—much better than the stuff we used to drink in college. When I knocked, no one answered. I figured she was out somewhere and maybe I could find that letter before she got back. I didn't need to worry. She was on the bed. Dead."

He shook his head. "So, I took my time. I tore that place apart but couldn't find it. The only thing I saw that could connect us was that photo on the wall. That stupid picture of the six of us. We all had a print. I kept mine, of course, but I didn't think anyone else would still have a copy. Told you she was a hoarder. I smashed the frame and ripped it out. But I still needed that letter. I could almost feel it. I knew it was there—somewhere in that cluttered mess. And I knew that if someone found it—well, it wouldn't be good. So," he shrugged. "I used the brandy to light the fire. There was enough paper and shit around that once it got going, I knew it would destroy everything."

He paused, took a deep breath, seemed to pull himself out of his memory. He looked down at me. His eyes narrowed, and I knew he was back and that he was done telling stories. He reached out and grabbed my hand. "Now it's your turn to talk. I want to know what my wife told you. I need to know what she knew." He squeezed.

I gasped. Strange as it seems, I welcomed the excruciating pain because it kept the sleeping meds at bay. "Larry, let go of me. Honest, I told you everything I know."

"You little liar." This time he gave my hand a rough tug. "I know she talked to you. I know her. I know how she loves...loved to brag. She told you things. If you want to go peacefully, drop the act and tell me the truth." He leaned in closer and he spat his words. "Or, I swear..."

I gathered every bit of strength I could and lobbed my right fist straight at his nose. Missed. My punch landed on his chin with a crack. I tried again and struck out. I started to scream.

"You bitch! Shut up!" He slapped my face, let go of my hand, and smashed his palm over my mouth. He tugged at the pillow.

I squirmed. My legs tangled in the sheets. I turned my head—he pressed down harder. I tried to reach up and scratch him, but when I did, he gave the pillow a tug, and it came free. He jammed it over my face and pushed it down on my nose. I couldn't catch a breath. I tried to suck air into my mouth and got only the rough cotton of hospital linen. I flailed around—tried to kick free from the sheets—made fists and struck wildly. I felt one blow land somewhere on his face but I was losing air and I knew there wasn't much drive behind the punch.

"Fucking bitch!" He pushed down harder.

My world grew dim, then dark. My energy ebbed. I had one, fleeting thought—water. Shimmering light twinkling on deep, blue water.

"Stop! Hands up!" A woman's voice.

Lawrence released the pillow. I grabbed at it, pulled it from my face, and gasped for air. A loud crack blasted by my head. Then another. Explosions of sound and light. Then something hot and wet splattered across my face.

# 32

The sound of those guns, his and the policewoman's, reverberated in my skull for hours. The cops interviewed me for days—going over and over the few minutes Larry had been at my bedside. It took weeks for the nurses to move me to a new room and for me to wash the blood and bits of Larry's flesh from my face and hair. Weeks. At least that's how it seemed at the time. Everything happened in slow motion—the pillow over my face, the darkness, the shots. In reality, the whole thing went down in a flash.

The policewoman who'd sat quietly taking notes during my chats with Lilly, the cop who'd helped transport gift balloons and potted plants from my hospital room, the officer who'd come back to collect the notebook she'd accidentally left on my bedside table, was the woman who'd returned in time to save my life. Larry had tried to take hers, but he was a shitty shot. She was not.

"Look, you're okay now." She smiled and motioned for me to turn around so she could give me a hand with the clean hospital gown. "We've posted an officer outside your door. The chances of anyone else trying to harm you is highly unlikely." She swept my wet hair off my shoulders and quickly tied the gown closed. Then she extended her hand and helped me climb into bed.

"What about Elaine Dupont?" I asked. "She's involved somehow. I know that for sure—I just can't put it together right now."

"We have her in custody. And you're right. She was involved. I'll explain everything in a couple of days. I still need to ask you more questions, but you don't have to think about anything else tonight. Try to get some rest. Remember, tomorrow is a big day—you're going to your new home."

"Home? New home?" In all the confusion I'd forgotten that I'd be released from the hospital in the morning. I'd forgotten that Lilly had a secret—something special. I'd forgotten that Lilly had a plan.

The officer smiled and winked. "I promised your friend not to spill the details. But I can tell you, it's charming. You're going to be very happy there. Now, get some rest."

Shortly after the policewoman left, the night nurse arrived. The young woman who normally handled the shift had been replaced with a charming, dark-haired man.

"Hi," he smiled and held out his hand. "Ray. Remember me, now? *Evergreen Gardens?* The Retirement Home? Your friend, Lilly? We're uh..." His face turned a deep pink and he hurried on. "I picked up some extra hours here at the hospital when Lilly told me what happened to you. She feels better knowing I'm here. Can I bring you some hot tea or a cup of cocoa?"

Lilly. Ray. I *did* remember him, and I remembered how Lilly had almost swooned whenever he'd come into the hospital room on rounds—more likely to see her than anything to do with me or his job. As far as I could tell, he and Lilly were a good match—age-appropriate, obviously crushing on each other, and he was probably a stabilizing influence on my flighty friend. Plus, he was doing his best to make me feel safe. Any other time I would have joked around—just for the game of it. However, at that moment, the only thing I wanted was to sleep. I'd never wanted, so much, to sleep. I wanted to sink into that comfortable place of no memories, no dreams, no thoughts of any kind—if only for one more night.

"Okay, Ray," I said. "Thanks. Um...I did take a sleeping pill a while ago, but I'm not sure..."

"Already ahead of you." He grinned and held up a small paper cup. "Called your doc and filled her in. She suggested this." He handed the cup to me along with a glass of water, and then moved to fluff my pillow.

I flinched.

He pulled back—fast—looked embarrassed. "Oh, God, I'm so sorry. I didn't even think." He thrust his hands into the pockets of his scrubs.

I sighed. "It's okay. I'm just jumpy and really tired."

We spent a couple more minutes being extra polite to each other, but he kept his distance from the bed. He chatted about Lilly and he told me how he'd helped her move when the city tore the eggplant down. He mentioned that they'd donated the concrete animals to a daycare center and that the children loved climbing on the heavy "pets." I knew he was doing his job and waiting for the meds to kick in. Finally, he nodded toward the door.

"Guessing that cop lady mentioned that they've put an officer on guard for the night. No one will come in here, except me. And..." He paused a moment, swallowed, looked uncomfortable. Even though the light was low, I could see that his face flushed. "If you'd rather have a different nurse—a female, I can trade shifts. No worries."

I tried to manage a smile. "Oh Ray, that's sweet. No need to switch. It's great having you around. Between you and that officer, well, I couldn't feel any safer."

He exhaled. "Good. I'll do my best to..." He didn't need to finish his sentence. I knew he'd been assigned to me not only for his nursing skills but to add another male presence around my room. Hadn't the hospital staff noticed it was a female who'd protected me earlier? A woman who'd saved my life? A rant tried to stir, but grogginess pushed it aside. Maybe another time.

"All right," Ray said, "if you need anything, use the buzzer. You're my only patient tonight. I'll come running."

I tried my best to offer a genuine and appreciative smile, but I felt myself drifting as Ray left the room. He'd pulled a shade over the window, leaving a thin strip of light under the door, and the faint digital glow from the call button draped over the rail of my bed to fend off darkness. The room was still and silent, the scent of disinfectant lingered in the air. I sighed and turned my face toward the wall. And then, it happened. I had expected to drift into a deep, medically induced sleep. Instead, I drifted into a silent movie. A movie with sepia-toned scenes that played out in halting slow motion. Scenes that ran together—tangled events and episodes out of logical order.

There was Bud, grinning from ear to ear, pulling himself up and into *Ink Spot's* cockpit. My heart clenched as I saw Chen, reaching over to brush a strand of hair from my face, his eyes shining. I could almost feel his warm breath. I saw Geraldine's bone-thin finger tracing the lines of her painting—her painting of a man in a business suit standing on the deck of a dilapidated floating home. And there was a barrel of a shiny gun—big as a fist—pointed at my chest. Finally, I saw a flash of light so bright it blinded me. My back arched as I felt myself lifting upward. Flying. Then nothing. That's when my memories stopped.

And that's when my emotions kicked in. They came with the strength of a storm as I realized—truly understood—for the first time since waking in the hospital, that my beloved *Ink Spot* was gone. Forever, gone. I'm not someone who lets her emotions take over, at least not often. But at that moment the tears came in a flood and soaked my hair and the pillow. I sobbed, without a sound, until there was nothing left—no fear, no pain, no grief, just my heart pumping slow like waves at low tide.

## The Second Full Moon

We were all there. Dorothy pushed Charlie around in his wheelchair. Geraldine clutched a plastic bonnet in case of rain. Desmond's five little dogs ran in circles, barking, wagging, and tangling their leads around his legs. Lilly and Ray held hands. Oh yes, Che and the other skateboard boys—they were with us, too. And we were all stoned. We figured the best way to honor Shirley was a massive celebration of her life, so we rented Seattle's premiere party boat, the *Argosy*, hired a caterer, and booked a band. And we finished off the last of her magic brownies.

Apparently, Seattle has some sort of law prohibiting the dispersal of human remains—in any form—in the lake. And so, we snuck Shirley's ashes aboard in small sandwich bags. We all got one—a little piece of Shirley. Because there wasn't anything left of Bud, we printed up a huge photo of him, burned it, and brought those ashes along as well. We figured we'd party until dark and then fling the dusty remains of our friends overboard. Then, in their honor, we'd party some more.

When I hadn't been planning Shirley's celebration, or trying to rebuild my physical strength, I'd spent a lot of time sitting on Geraldine's deck thinking about Chen's offer. I'd imagine myself at the wheel of a new SUV driving giggling girls to sleepovers. I saw myself listening during parent/teacher meetings. I'd thought about cooking, and cleaning, and planning family vacations. Then, I'd look out and see a sailboat glide past with its solitary captain at the wheel. I'd see that sailor squinting up to the wind vane working to catch the perfect breeze. And I knew I wasn't ready—yet—for Girl Scouts, the baking of cupcakes, or a yard.

A week after we'd had "the talk," I'd called Chen and asked if he and Willow would like to fly up for Shirley and Bud's celebration of life. They could stay with Geraldine and me, you know, as friends. Chen had thanked me but had begged off—lots of father/daughter activities to do before the school year started.

"Maybe another time," he'd added.

I had considered burning his handkerchief and sending it out, across the lake, with Shirley and Bud. It had survived the blast by being tucked in the pocket of my jeans when I'd been blown off *Ink Spot*. I'd also thought about burning the note he'd written to me. It had come home from the hospital still tucked in the pages of a paperback. But while I didn't get the feeling I should hold my breath waiting for "another time," that note and his handkerchief were the only physical reminders of my former life—my life before the explosion. I couldn't part with them.

The band struck up the chorus of "YMCA"—that silly little tune that begs a smile and a happy dance every time you hear it.

"Come on, Blue!" Lilly tugged at my shirt. "Let's conga!" She grinned wide and bopped her head in time to the music.

While Lilly has always been contented in a Namaste-sort-of-way, I'd never seen her this happy. The city had given her some cash for the Quonset hut—not much, but enough to pay off her bills and start fresh. She'd managed to secure a full-time job driving the van at Charlie's old retirement home, and when she wasn't chauffeuring seniors to community events, she was teaching them to salsa or to swing dance.

While Shirley didn't have a policy with City Wide, she did have one with another—more reputable—agency. Her life insurance policy paid out way more than we could have imagined.

The beneficiaries were Greenpeace, Amnesty International, The Humane Society, and the Dock W Homeowners Association. Charlie had used his accounting skills to create a budget for the money, and there was enough to help everyone live comfortably, enough to pay my hospital bills, and enough to make Dock W look brand new. Charlie even found a way to buy me another used car, since the cost to get Roger out of hock turned out to be more than the old Volvo was worth.

With help from the skateboard boys, Ray built a wheelchair ramp and Charlie returned home to his houseboat which he, Ray, and Lilly now share. A local Habitat for Humanity group turned Shirley's empty slip into a floating community garden. When they'd completed their work and left the dock, the boys added a smattering of not-for-medicinal-use, just-for-personal-fun, pot plants cleverly placed among sunflowers and hollyhocks. And finally, when Lilly wasn't working at the retirement home, or taking care of Charlie, she and Ray were taking care of each other. Like they were now.

Ray had his arm twisted around her waist and was already swiveling his hips in time to the beat. "Yeah, come on. As your personal medical advisor, I hereby declare you fit enough to conga!"

I grinned at the couple. They'd obviously scored in the "finding the one" department. I thought about Chen and felt a stab of pain. "Thanks," I said, "but I think I'll just enjoy the ride for the moment."

Ray shrugged and swept Lilly off to join the others in the dance.

I took one more look at my friends as they hopped and bumped and laughed along together before I turned and leaned on the *Argosy's* railing. We traveled along Seattle's shoreline in a slow, no-wake journey around the lake. I sucked in the crisp scent of early evening. A light breeze lifted my hair and brushed it from my face. It wasn't exactly sailing, but still, time on the water is always better than time on land.

I thought of *Ink Spot*. It was almost impossible to even breathe her name without having my heart clench. I pushed the feeling away by remembering the Duponts and their vicious battle for power...over what? Power over what?

Elaine had wanted to rule the Seattle waterfront. Or at least a little slice of it. It hadn't been enough that at one time, her father had been a port commissioner, and that she had inherited great wealth. She'd tried to use some of her wealth to buy a Seattle police officer—tried to get him to push the button on an explosive device attached to a rental car. But Seattle police are neither gullible nor corrupt. The trial for her role in the death of Bud and the attempted murder of me and Detective David Chen was scheduled for late spring. We would all be there.

Lawrence Winslow, and his wife, Beverly, had been blown to bits. Different places, different methods, but still, both blown to bits. Served them right. I hoped they were screaming in Hell. Lilly tried to counsel me into a state of forgiveness, but I didn't plan on going there, not for a while anyway. Do the math—between them, Lawrence Winslow, his wife, and her mother had killed a port commissioner, a wonderful, feisty woman, and a sweet, elderly gentleman. They had tried to kill the first man I thought...well, maybe.... Not only that, Lawrence had tried to kill me. And Beverly—that bitch, that harpy—had destroyed my beautiful *Ink Spot*. Like I said, I hoped they were screaming in Hell.

I didn't get to sail down to Zihuatanejo or get to sleep away my days in a hammock under a palm tree. Instead, I moved into Geraldine's houseboat. She didn't need or want rent money from me, which was a good thing, because I didn't have a job. City Wide lost its biggest client and went out of business. To his credit, Glen Broom gave me a small severance check. I spent it on post-hospital self-medication and on Shirley's celebration of life. Geraldine was content if I simply kept her company and took her to buy art supplies whenever she needed them. Her friends were happy that I watched over her and made sure she didn't wander off. The three of them—Dorothy, Geraldine, and Charlie—shared their singular greatest wish. They only wanted to spend their golden years, peacefully, in their own homes.

I'd always figured the way I wanted to die would be on a trip over the transom, in some warm, tropical sea, while snot-slinging drunk on good, Tennessee whiskey. But after what happened with Shirley, and Bud, and *Ink Spot,* I wasn't so sure.

I looked up to the sky. The sun had set, the moon was rising, and a few stars were bright enough to twinkle over the water. The breeze was cool, and I shivered. We cruised past the houseboats and I squinted to see Geraldine's little blue home at the end of Dock W. We always left a light on so it was easy to see the silhouette of one lucky cat. His head pointed skyward—he watched us sail by. Or maybe, he howled at a pale blue moon.

# ACKNOWLEDGMENTS

Special thanks to the fine writers of the Bellingham, Washington, Red Wheelbarrow Writers and the Fridays Only Critique Group. Grateful appreciation to Chanticleer International Book Awards and to Black Magnolia Books for the encouragement and the awards. Credit to the guys at the gun counter at Dave's Sports Shop in Lynden, Washington, for help with all brain-splatter matters. Huge thanks to Sidekick Press for inspiration, order, soup, and cookies. Thanks to my Cousin Pam—her laughter keeps me sane. And, as always, gratitude to my critters who remind me that joy is the meaning of life.

# ABOUT THE AUTHOR

Photo by Jolene Hanson

Jessica H. Stone (Jes) is a blue water sailor and the food dispensing unit for a brave and boisterous dog and a sleek Siamese cat. She collects fountain pens and lives in a pretty little town by the sea.

Learn more at jessicahstone.com.

CPSIA information can be obtained
at www.ICGtesting.com
Printed in the USA
FSHW011301150621
82405FS